1 DOWN 4 UP

Rejoin - Rejoice - Re-Joan

Cathy Formusa

BookLocker

Trenton, Georgia

Published by BookLocker.com, Inc., Trenton, Georgia.

BookLocker.com, Inc.
2024

First Edition

Library of Congress Cataloguing in Publication Data
Formusa, Cathy
1 DOWN 4 UP: Rejoin - Rejoice - Re-Joan by Cathy Formusa
Library of Congress Control Number: 2024902780

Dedicated to Mom
who applauds and encourages adventures.
Like this one.

Thanks to Garbage Guy, to Spoolie, and to Gary.
Thanks to my guides, 'The Guys', and
Thanks to your guides that led you here.

GRAM and PA

Joan tiptoed down the short hallway and peeked from behind the wooden pantry that smelled pleasantly of cinnamon. He is stirring something, maybe sugar, maybe milk into it; she didn't know his ways or his things yet. The sound of the spoon going round and round, knocking the ceramic cup now and then, was a comforting sound. The sun was up and shining through the window above the sink, across Gram's sky-blue tablecloth on the small round table and onto Grandpa's hands that nestled his coffee cup. She could see from where she stood that his hands were covered with deep wrinkles and spots. "He's going to go too and maybe soon," she thought to herself.

Suddenly, Joan began to feel wrapped in cold shivers and weakness. This felt like a fast one to her. Her knees couldn't control it now, and when the memories began to flash like a movie playing fast-forward, Joan quickly sat on the cool tile floor to wait it out. The cold covered her like a cloak, and she immediately listened for a sound to grab quickly. She clung onto Gram's refrigerator's buzzing like a life ring. Her focus on it kept her from sinking lower. She remembered to breathe steadily and deeply. Her left arm held both her legs to her chest, her right hand placed over Saturn, the name she gave the large planet-shaped scar on her lower leg and held it there to remind herself to focus. The buzzing sounded like monks chanting." This is now, it's over," she thought. The shouting and various tones of voices screaming at once now. Overtaken by the darkness inside the smelly smoke, holding her leg and wondering what happened. There was another strange smell mixed in there that would come and go, it wasn't a smokey smell. This time, Joan spotted something new; she saw a Fireman in the smoke walking towards her. Joan squeezed her body into a tight curl with one cheek on the knee of her soft cotton pajama bottoms, and they felt wonderful. She rocked back and forth until she felt hot all over; that's when it would stop, she knew from experience.

Joan popped her eyes open and glanced around in a panic, but Grandpa hadn't moved from his spot. Relieved, she reminded herself once again, "I'm okay, I'm okay, I'm okay. It wouldn't happen ever again. It's a memory. It happened then, not now." She calmed her breathing to a steady pace, stood up, and headed into the kitchen for her first full day of living there.

"Grandpa?"

"Pa," he corrected Joan.

"Pa," she told herself and turned to look out the kitchen window. The warm sun on her face felt great, and she relaxed a little more. Being with Pa alone in the same room was special. It was quiet. She liked quiet; it gave her time to think, and she had a lot of thinking to do this summer.

"Pa, do you mind if I go look at your garage?"

"Shed," he corrected.

"Shed," Joan repeated. "Is it okay?"

"Anytime you want, Joanie. You go right ahead. Be careful of the things that are high up. How about some cereal?"

"Joan," Joan corrected, caught his eyes and smiled.

The screen door opened, and Grandma brought in a basket of vegetables from her garden with a rush of chilly morning air.

"Good morning, Grandma! Do you need help with that?"

Joan spoke softly, taking a couple of big steps to peek into the garden basket. She knew she wouldn't be able to do much, being new here, but wanted to be polite. She spotted raspberries and snatched one right away. "Hmm."

"G'morning, lil' one, my Invincible Saint Joan, how you likin' the wild Northwest?"

Pa coughed. "I think this one is from your side of the gene pool, darlin'. She already asked if it'd be all right to go exploring."

Gram asked Joan, "Now, Joanie my Spumoni, would you like to help me scramble up some of these eggs for us?"

Joan nodded, happy to be a part of something she could learn and help with, although she hadn't had any real experience with cooking more complicated than a salad. Back East, meals in New York were usually brought home because the variety was amazing and fun to explore, cheaper and faster than grocery shopping too. Occasionally she and her mom would cook up a casserole. Tuna-noodle with lots of breadcrumbs toasted on top was her favorite. She was nervous about helping and she had never seen dirty vegetables straight out of a garden before. The carrots had long greens attached and a string root at the other end. She was fascinated and scrutinizing the vegetables for a while when she realized the kitchen had gone silent. The two of them were smiling and watching her in stillness. She blushed and smiled.

"I guess you and your mom don't garden there in New York City, eh?" Gram laughed, hugging Joan's side and looking into the basket with Joan. "You are in for a treat from the garden this summer. It's a good year."

Joan had no idea what a "good year" meant, but from the celebratory tone of Gram's voice, she was looking forward to finding out.

Pa nodded back. "You be sure to change into some sturdy work clothes before you go exploring around here, young lady. You'll be fine, but this isn't the city; we have—"

"Yes, Pa," Joan smiled, and Pa nodded once with a wink. Joan decided first she'd make breakfast with Gram and then change out of her pajamas and into the day.

Grandma said, "I hear that Doris is staying home from summer camp this summer for her diving. She said there are openings still for more kids at ArtCamp." Grandma looked at Joan. "Do you want to do ArtCamp this summer, Joan?

Joan shrugged, "Um, maybe? I don't know yet, okay Gram?"

"You betcha. We can talk 'bout that again, JoanBUG." Grandma winked, handing Joan a large wire whisk and bringing the bowl with eggs to the small table for Joan to scramble at a comfortable level.

Joan struggled to hold a confident face as she was a bit nervous being watched by Pa but scrambled up those eggs just fine in Pa's opinion. He watched her carefully, and she could feel him doing just that.

From Pa's years working with men from all walks of life in the construction business, he developed a keen sense of what someone is made of, how they move their body, how they handle themselves in the company of others, and how they communicate. He believed that how we do and what we do on the outside reflects what's going on inside us.

After delicious eggs, toast, and jam, Joan opened the squeaky door to her bedroom and rifled through the suitcase and stack of clothes already unpacked into a ready position for a drawer decision of hers later, when the mood was right.

"I better stack my bones up and wander 'round with the 3-in-1 today, or that door will drive us crazy soon enough." Pa groaned as he rose from his chair.

With jeans, her hiking boots, a long-sleeved shirt, scarf, and vest for the lingering chill, Joan returned to the kitchen. Pa stood with his back leaning on the kitchen counter stirring honey into his coffee. He was facing Gram who was washing the breakfast dishes. He had just said something that made her laugh, and he held a long smile.

Joan always took her time observing people when she could. She had learned that people revealed a lot about themselves through the expressions they wore and how they carried themselves. Lots of hospital time had taught her weird things like that. It might not win her any prizes, Joan figured, but she considered it a talent.

Pa looked up. "Will this do for exploring?" Joan stood in front of him, awaiting his attention.

"Yesindeedee," Pa replied as Joan turned to head out. "Remember what I said about being careful of the -"

The kitchen screen door slapped behind her as Joan stepped off the small landing of the back porch. She walked out into the day, thinking, "This is my new home for the summer. This is it for now. I'm okay with this." The sun felt wonderful on her face. In the field beyond Grandma's garden, steam was rising here and there. "This is beautiful," she thought. "I'm okay."

Turning the faucet off, Gram shook her head, "Each time we see her, she seems more fragile than the time before. Pa. I'm so happy she's here. With us."

Pa turned around and stepped behind Gram at the sink. He looked over her head through the kitchen window and kissed the top of her head. They both watched Joan bounce up from looking at something on the ground near Gram's garden fence, most likely deer poop Gram thought, and walk towards Pa's shed in the distance where the driveway curved around the house. Joan reached her hand out, touching the large, shady hazelnut tree as she went, and Pa raised his hand resting it on Gram's shoulder with a tender squeeze. "Hm," he remarked, "He was about her age when we all planted that tree, wasn't he?"

"Oh, yes," Gram responded softly, gazing out at Joan, filling the day.

He gave her another kiss atop her head, "We'll keep an eye on her, and we'll need to know how she's doing," Pa said, squeezing Gram's shoulders. "The ArtCamp school thing is a good idea. It'll be okay. We'll be good for her. We are just what she needs. Two old farts, some boredom, and a simple routine." He kissed the top of her head again.

"She sure reminds me of him," Gram said softly. The room itself seemed to pause for a moment.

"Inside that young lady is a confidence no bigger than a minnow in a fishing pond, I think is what we have here. Time here will do wonders. Before we know it, we'll be needing to catch up."

Gram turned around and reached around Pa, squeezing herself into a hug. "I miss him so," Gram muffled into Pa's chest. "It's a miracle we didn't lose them both."

PONY

At first, Joan didn't think much of all the strange tools and greasy stuff she found in Pa's shed. Her first awareness was that this was the place to be when it was hot out. The concrete floor radiated cool up through her shoes as she moved on, with bits of breeze easing their way through the shed's wrinkled wooden planked walls just fine here and there. This feels very different from the Gram's clean house, that's for sure, more comfortable too. Something secret about it too, like a place with no rules. Standing here and there is a menagerie of wood in all sorts of sizes and shapes, usually rectangles. Large planks were lying across the rafters. The more she looked at one area the more she admired how much Pa could store in that space. Above her lay tubular plastic things, rods, sawhorses folded and stored, long pieces of all kinds of material and even a small round seat stored up there.

Enough time had passed that the concrete floor had dissolved itself into crumbs and flat, old dirt as hard as a street. Things in her so-called path, a path of her slowly turning, shifting, taking a step this way and that, seemed to have a reason they were left there. These things all had stories to tell, Joan thought. The deeper she walked in the more she loved this place. She had been to hardware stores, and she had looked under the hood of a car and truck, but this was special. "Oh!" aloud, Joan surprised herself; she thought of it. Of course, this felt special; it was a lifetime of Pa here.

Now and then the sun would peek in through a large crack in one of the shed's wallboards and slivers of sunshine would shine upon this and that. In one spot she noticed a broken wallboard made a small square natural window. She smiled; it felt like the air in there reached out and was hugging her. She'd move a box or can out of her way to walk further and she'd smell something new, in this spot earthy, in this spot heavy. She was feeling tingly, excited and didn't know why. This place smells like it's one big bunch of PA flowers!

The shed was kind of like Pa, old but still standing strong. It seemed like he knew what to do with it all because it seemed to have some order and care put into it. Some things were put together in teams of whatever they do. Some areas were messy like it didn't matter much, while other areas were neatly arranged, ready for some action. She liked that mystery. She liked it in here more and more and she felt closer to Pa now too. He didn't seem so quiet here. All his things seemed to want to say something if they could. It made sense to Joan that Gram had her garden, and this was Pa's garden.

Against the back wall was a large section of stacked cans. Small, larger, some spray paints. She'd only seen this many cans in one place at a hardware store until now. There were paints, varnishes, oils, things she couldn't even guess what they were for. She walked slowly deeper into the shed, passing that wall of canned stuff, and stopped at another workbench along the wall. Above it hung a shelf with glass baby food jars hung by their lids attached to the underside of the shelf. He had nailed the lids to the bottom of the board so that he could screw the jar up and into the lids. "Genius!" Joan said aloud. Every jar had something in it. She recognized a jar of tiny screws, one of washers and nuts, one of ball bearings. Most of the little labels were worn off in some fashion, but she could make out one labeled "Bananas," and inside was a tiny toy banana. "HA!" Joan exclaimed aloud. In all this crazy stuff, there is Pa's humor too! Joan thought.

Something scurried near her feet, and she quickly looked around a box to catch sight. That's when her eyes caught something peeking out at her eye level from under a thick tarp covered in little speckles and big blotches of paints and stains just on the other side of a large support post. A sun ray was hitting the small round shiny thing, and it flickered as if it was saying a silent hello. She could see its shape, it was metal, and the rest of it was a huge mound under the tarp. She made her way over thinking maybe it was a bicycle, but knew it was too big for that. She peeked under and slowly pulled the tarp off. It had a denser smell than the rest of the shed, having been under the tarp, and she liked the smell even more. It was so different; it was exciting. It made sense having its own smell. We all do, all things. She thought that was an interesting thought.

"Well, helllllllloooo, you are coooool," Joan whispered as her eyes gazed at the motorcycle. She touched its seat and stepped on the dusty tarp as she walked around it, feeling its different shapes and thicknesses of metal, chrome, and steel. She held its handlebar and gave it a push to check its strength. Joan just stood beside the motorcycle, although it was obviously old and banged up, it was bringing her such joy to have found it. She didn't know why it was amazing to her; it just seemed like a life unto itself. She realized she was smiling and wanted to make it smile too. "You've been under this tarp a long time I bet," Joan patted the seat as if the old machine was a pet. She found the small peg sticking out of the side, and so with another tug and push, she decided it was safe enough and lifted one leg over and leaned naturally forward into a riding position. Her body fit the motorcycle perfectly, legs on each side with feet resting in a riding position. She had no idea what the levers and pedals did, but she knew she wanted to find out.

Having been taught to put things back where she found them at an early age, she hesitantly did just that, covering the small round mirror as well to keep it from further damage. Nodding, knowing she wanted this, she said aloud, "I'll be back!" She said aloud to the covered mound and zigzagged around and away from the back of the shed carefully but with some speed, mostly internally, and her mind raced. Carefully, but faster, not to rush out of the shed, sure she couldn't risk making any mistakes or hurting herself or anything else. Her body was getting wildly giddy within. She promised to be careful, and she knew she needed all the help she could get with what she was about to ask. She wanted the whole story, and she wanted a ride. She wanted to ride it alone too. She wanted it somehow. Well, she didn't know, but she wanted more, and come to think of it, she thought, she hadn't "wanted" anything in a long time and there was excitement for the first time in a really long time, since the attack, she knew for sure.

In front of the shed, she stood at the edge of the concrete pad, under the slight overhang and looked across the field to the house. She looked around, allowing the trees and bushes to hand off her gaze as if they were all shaking hands to greet her to their place, a welcoming. Something just happened, something good, she could feel it. She couldn't put it into words if someone had asked her to, but she knew it felt comfortable.

"I'm okay," she took a deep breath, tilted her head into the sun and enjoyed the warmth on her skin.

Joan dashed from the shed past Gram, who was back in her garden of fluffy dark black dirt and the sun sparkled on the top of her garden hat. Joan spotted Pa and quickened her step to a jog. Pa was out front talking into a mail truck. She wanted to be mature about this and somehow make a deal, any deal, to make this become something real for her, but it was too late. Her excitement overran any approach under control by this point. It seemed that somehow the motorcycle and discovering Pa's shed had built up to an enormous burst of the word, "PA!" Joan called out running up to him, out of breath.

She tried to calm herself now and was a little embarrassed by her outburst, knowing she should be patient and polite in front of adults.

"Wow, who is this?"

"Blaise, this is-

"Hi, I'm Joan," she said, extending her hand for a handshake. Blaise smiled and did the same.

"She'll be staying with us while her mom is deployed over in Iraq for the summer," Pa said.

"Hey welcome Joan! I hope I get to deliver you some smiles to keep yours as beautiful as the one you are wearing today. See you around the neighborhood. Take it easy Francis." Blaise smiled at Joan and drove off over the gravel towards her next stop.

"Thanks, Blaise," Pa said sardonically.

"Francis? Is that your real name? Wow, I didn't know your name was Francis!"

"Alright, that's the last time I hear you say it, young lady," Pa put his arm around the top of Joan's shoulders, gave

her a pat, and they walked back towards the house. "What's got your teeth grinning so wide?"

"Pa, I—" Joan slowed down. She reminded herself THIS was important. She knew from the hospital that when she wanted the authorities to really listen to her, she'd slow down to make them take note.

"Pa, I found it, in the shed, under the tarp. It's beautiful. It had its ear sticking out and I saw it, then I saw all of it."

"What's what, what Joan, what are you saying?"

"The mo-tor-cy-cle," Joan pronounced it slow and drawn out to show her excitement and mimicking as if she was riding it and its meaningfulness to her. "Can I ride it? I fit it great, I reach the pedals and"-

She's not getting a reaction, maybe that's a 'no', she thinks to herself and switches her own gears, "Can you take me for a ride? Pa? I love it!"

"Ohhh," he nodded, then took a few thought-filled steps. "You met my Pony." He patted her shoulder. "She's an old broken-down Pony, and she isn't running."

"Pa, can you fix her up? I can help you. I don't know how, but I can!"

He tilted his head then gave it a shake, "Too many years ago. I think she might be frozen up, and if not, there is so much to do that I don't think she's got anything left in her. Not too sure I do either. No, she's out to pasture now."

"Let's do it, Pa! Let's do it!" Joan interrupted, unable to hold back the excitement that this was really a possibility.

"She's got rust in areas that- well, I'd have to look her over. But after all these years—"

"Let's do it, Pa! Could we do it together? I'd love to learn that stuff in your shed, and she smells so good, Pa!" Joan surprised herself by telling him that she felt a little naked.

Pa laughed, "I know what you mean by the smell; sometimes it's like being in a different world when I go in there. I'm glad you like it."

There was a long pause; they both looked at the ground as they walked a few steps. Then Pa said, "If it isn't froze-up, well, it means ordering parts, cleaning all the rust, who knows how deep that's crept in. It could be miserable for you. I don't think—"

"I don't care about rust, I can handle rust, I don't mind the hard work. I was all rusted and broken once and I got fixed up!" Joan threw both arms pointing at her lower leg. "Let's do it, Pa. Can we, please?"

Pa walked around the side of the house with Joan at his side. She was all wiggle-worm under his arm resting on her shoulder as they walked on. At the sight of the shed and in sight of Gram in her garden, Pa spoke louder, "I don't know, Joan, it's a huge commitment, could take all summer. I think your ArtCamp would be a whole lot easier for you and for me as well."

Gram heard them now and leaned back up, watching them from the upside-down bucket she used to sit on while tending the weeds and such.

They were back at the shed. He was shaking his head with eyebrows raised now. He was still holding on to a corner of the tarp they removed.

"Paahhhhh!" Joan had her arms outstretched displaying her smile and the motorcycle between the two of them. "We can do it."

"This Pony," Pa winced, still shaking his head. He covered up the old motorcycle and Joan's face dropped from hope to sadness. He was shaking his head as they made their way back out to the front of the shed. He looked over at Gram, who threw him a frown and a shake of her head mouthing,'NO!." Pa looked at the both of them, Gram was now ignoring them, not wanting Joan to know she was discouraging this idea secretly to Pa. Pa scratched the back of his neck and then looked down at Joan who was looking off in the distance with a quiet sadness written on her face. Pa smiled back at Gram past Joan, "I guess anything's possible if you throw a lot of hard work and love into it," he broke the silence smiling at Joan who whipped her head around and up into his eyes with shock. He rolled his eyes. He put both his hands on her shoulders and leaned down close. He glanced quickly at Gram and motioned over at her, who was still holding a frown at him. He quietly said to Joan, "Now really," he whispered, "the person you have to ask isn't me. I put my Pony in that corral because your Gram asked me to. It's not me you have to convince," he nodded in Gram's direction.

Joan locked Pa's eyes and nodded yes to Pa, understanding what was needed.

———

"Absolutely not. No. We almost lost her once in her lifetime and I don't want her risking her life out here on a motorcycle. You don't either. What were you thinking? No." Gram was washing carrots with a special scrubbing glove on her hand and talking to Pa while facing the kitchen window in front of her.

"Now hold on there, Sparky."

"No. No is a complete sentence."

"Whether or not we even get the Pony up and running again is a long shot. This might just be what the little monkey needs. It'll keep her occupied. She'll learn some useful mechanical knowledge. Boost her confidence. Joan won't be bored and get into trouble. That girl has more tomboy in her than cheerleader and she seems to already have some interest." He gave Gram a squeeze of the shoulders and reached for a glass of water giving his bride a kiss on her forehead as he brought the glass over to the sink where Gram was washing the newly grown green beans from the garden for tonight's meatloaf dinner, one of his favorites.

Gram rolled her eyes, gazed out the window in front of her, realizing this was not going to go her way. She did like the idea of the two of them bonding closer; Joan could use some guidance and confidence.

Gram's shoulders dropped. This was a tell for Pa that she was surrendering. "She's just turned 15, and she's a young 15. Years of in and out of the hospital, and now you want to put her back in—"

"It'll all work out," Pa interrupted her in a reassuring voice, "That pony has a lot of healing to do before we can even get her to cough." He hugged his bride tight into his chest, kissed the top of her head, and before she could say anything more, he bent down, looked straight into her eyes, and added, "She's a good kid, and we'll both be careful." He headed towards the door, grabbing his hat off the coat hook on the wall, turned back and added, "Oh, but play hard to get as hard as you want when she starts asking though; it's more fun that way," he winked and the screen door slapped behind him as he headed out to finish up the afternoon chores before dinner.

Gram laughed and let out a large "Ugh."

DORIS

Doris turned the corner, starting the curved downhill journey home and felt the familiar relief as the uphill pedal struggle ended. It was always a challenge for her quads to conquer 'Heart Attack Hill'. In fact, riding uphill was never easy for her, no matter the time or how great she felt.

Riding with no hands, she stretched her arms above her head, caught her breath and adjusted the still-wet towel hanging around her neck. The warm breeze indicated that summer was approaching. She took a deep breath trying to smell the jasmine in the air, but it was still too early, she surmised. Doris smiled as she coasted down the hill, navigating the bumps, potholes and gravel effortlessly. This was the downhill that encouraged her imagination to soar. The wind and speed this afternoon prompted a feeling of riding one of the creatures from the old movie 'Avatar.' Doris had a deep love for movies, any kind, and downhill rides often triggered thoughts of flying scenes from various films. She remembered 'Chitty-Chitty-Bang-Bang' after last Saturday's diving practice.

In a good dive, one with a long hang time in the air like a clean Forward, Back or even during a Full Reverse, Doris could briefly experience the sensation of flying. It was a dreamy feeling that gave her joyous goosebumps.

Doris grabbed the handlebars as she turned into the driveway and rode without pedaling, coasting down the long newly paved path on one pedal. She hopped off her bike and leaned against the porch corner.

She let out a long, loud whistle to her dad who was busy making noise in his workshop crafting metal into art. She waited for his response, knowing that shouting over the noise was impossible. Eventually, he acknowledged her with a similar whistle, their daytime communication system.

"Dad, I'm home."

"Great."

It was easier than texting him, as his hands were usually occupied with his work. They both enjoyed practicing loud whistles and creating different combinations, a source of laughter during meals together.

Doris had accepted her dad's limited technological knowledge and was content with their simple communication system. In their small town everyone knew each other or at least recognized each other well enough to help when needed. Doris found comfort in that, and her dad enjoyed the sense of community.

Doris' mom was on her 48-hour hospital shift, which meant they had some uninterrupted freedom. Doris was deeply engrossed in creating her second vision board after the first one had remarkably come true. She marked the validation dates when each item on the board became a reality, and now she looked forward to concentrating on her new vision board for the next couple of days.

She hung her towel on the hook inside the front door, kicked off her shoes, and walked across the soft, large throw rug into the kitchen. She grabbed a pizza from the freezer and noticed her mom had left her a note.

"Dodo, I think this is the week Joan arrives. Welcome her, okay? Text me. I love you."

"Cool!" Doris was curious about Joan. They hadn't seen each other for years, but they had been close when they were kids, or at least she remembered it that way. Since the bombs, they had lost touch completely. The idea of hanging out together again this summer excited her, and she hoped Joan felt the same. Much had changed since they last met, but they were neighbors, so a renewed friendship would be a bonus.

Apart from the National memorial for lives lost in the bombings, the town also had a memorial for Joan's dad, primarily for his surviving parents and neighbors. Doris recalled that Joan and her mom weren't there. She had heard that Joan was recovering, but she didn't know the details. Now, Joan was returning, and Doris looked forward to catching up and hearing her story.

Doris put the pizza in the oven and walked over to the window with a view of the trees towards Gram and Pa's place. She wondered what Joan might look like now and how the incident had changed her. Would she be scarred? Would it be unsettling to see her? Doris had many questions, and she hoped Joan would be open to reconnecting. She decided to visit her after dinner.

Opening the front door, she listened for a break in her dad's noisy work and then let out two loud whistles to signal "Dinnertime!"

NEIGHBORS

The rain relaxed into puddles the next morning, light enough to motivate Doris off her computer and head across to meet up with Joan. That's the thing about the Northwest, there is a saying "If you don't like the weather, stick around five minutes." But last night it just didn't want to let up. Showers just before summer are common, just as an early summer frost tricks those early planted vegetable gardens, usually planted by any newbies in town.

"Dad, I'm heading over to Gram and Pa's to see Joan. See ya!" Doris called out as she threw her raincoat over her t-shirt and shorts, slipping on her green "Mudders." She knew he heard her, but it didn't really matter; it was Saturday, and her mom was gone. Double reason – no one expected to keep track of her whereabouts anyway. Doris was known for working as hard in her social and athletic activities as her excellent schoolwork. She had learned that the pressure she put on herself was enough for the whole family. With a clear goal in mind, she studied those who had 'made it,' reading their autobiographies, listening to interviews on YouTube, and reminding herself with quotes from successful people. Most people she shared a quote or two with took it with a smile.

"Meet up with your fears. If you're afraid of sharks, go learn all about sharks. Get into the water with one." -Laird Hamilton

She headed over and around to the back door, Gram's kitchen entrance. Gram liked people to take off their shoes, and to always use the wet room on rainy days; a common respect in town. To Doris, this was super smart; it meant less cleaning and she tried to get her dad to adopt the habit, but it was useless. She gave Gram props for sticking to training people about her floors.

"Heyyyyy" Doris called out in a funny tune as she opened the kitchen door; she never liked the sound of the way it slapped when you walked in so Doris always held the door as it shut.

"Dodo-Doris!" Gram smiled, "Are you hungry?" Gram was already doing the breakfast dishes; but that's Gram, so kind to not let that stop her from cooking up some food for a drop-in visitor.

"No thanks Gram, thank you though. Mom says Joan is here?"

"It's so good to see you, Doris," Gram said, wiping her hands dry on a kitchen towel, probably made by her. Gram lifted her chin, nodding towards the window. "Happy Summer, eh?" she laughed. "They are both in the shed. Once the rain let up, off they went. Good luck finding them in there and I'll let the police know where to start the search if I don't see you around. " She smiled.

Doris, like everyone else in town, knew Pa as the man who called nothing 'junk' unless HE found it useless. He had trained everyone to not throw things away but to bring them to him to repair, recycle for reuse by another if the original owner didn't want it back, or if it truly wasn't something he could make useful in some form he'd break it down for proper recycling of some sort.

Doris has watched the shed grow in size during her life and is not surprised. Pa was a natural talent for fixing things. Her favorite example is that he has always maintained the town's theater popcorn machine maintenance when needed; in return, he gets free popcorn for life. Doris benefits from an occasional big bag he'll bring her from town. Because she's his neighbor and seen in town more often, people will wave her down and hand her something to bring home to him. She has kept a list of the items she has hauled home on her bike for him. She thought to start the list while she was strapping the second waffle iron onto her bicycle to bring home. Both of Doris' Grandpas had died before she was born, so Pa was like her grandpa, and she has always thought he was awesome.

"Thanks Gram," Doris turned to leave but then stopped and leaned into the kitchen, "Gram, is she okay? Is there anything I need to know, you know, about Joan?"

"She's really good Dodo; fragile I think, as you can imagine right?"

"Yeah, geez." Doris thought about how she couldn't imagine being buried under rubble. She shivered and looked at Gram.

"Exactly." Gram said, looking into Doris' eyes and shaking her head. "Joan is amazing, DoDo, and it's really fun to have her here."

"Thanks, Gram, love ya!" Doris said through the screen door as she eased it closed.

"Love you too, DoDo." Gram finished the conversation as Doris was already hopping mud puddles to the shed.

SWINGING FOR THE FENCES

Doris was pumping her way up Heart Attack Hill enjoying the candy smell of the wild sweet peas when she realized her legs felt stronger lately. She has been pushing her dry-land and weight workouts for over a month now and it showed.

She had perfected her 1 1/2 pike on the low board and 2 1/2 tuck on the three meter, impressing her coach as well as other coaches who started attending practice more often. Everything seemed to fit right. She felt a new ease in her diving. Her friendship with her new neighbor Joan was flourishing and they had become close friends.

She had successfully convinced her school counselor that her springboard diving hours deserved as much credit as the ArtCamp summer hours that were credited toward her upcoming school year. She argued that diving involved physics and was an art form in itself; performance art. This achievement fueled her excitement as she pedaled home looking forward to seeing what Joan and Pa were up to today.

Doris reminisced about the day they first met again at almost halfway up Heart Attack Hill.

:::

"These things here are mostly in the way and not doing much more than that." Pa was saying to Joan. Doris could hear them but hadn't seen them yet inside the shed.

"Uh-huh." Joan nodded, scanning the cluttered shed for a place to relocate the items that Pa had identified as needing to be moved. Hope and Pa's attention were the only tools she had to work with.

"Heyyyy, it's me, Pa, you in here? Joan?"

Joan's head popped around one of the wooden shed's support posts with a smile. "HI!"

"Hi! I'm Doris, they call me Dodo. I don't remember you very much; we were so little, huh? Mom says we liked each other a lot, so that's good, right? I mean, uhm... hi."

"Hi, I'm Joan, nice to see you. *Again.* Ha, do you know Pa's motorcycle? He calls it his Pony." She pointed to Pa who was preoccupied with inspecting one end of some snake-shaped metal thing in his hands. Doris shook her head no.

"Hi, Dodo, you staying dry?"

"Wow, what a downpour. I think I saw Dad's cucumbers in a puddle doing the backstroke." Doris smiled, and Joan burst into laughter. "Wow, thanks for laughing." Doris smiled.

"You're funny! So, Pa and I are going to fix his Pony." Joan said with excitement. "Pa says we first have to find room to work."

"That's even funnier." Doris kidded, and they both laughed.

"Hey now, don't harsh my mellow." Pa smiled. Joan and Doris exchanged puzzled glances at what Pa found funny. Pa shook his head and focused back on his work, his eyes dancing with thought, and Joan watched him patiently.

A few minutes later Doris decided that this would make a great subject for documentation; an art form in itself. She explained to Joan that ArtCamp was a national program that could earn her school credits.

The following week, both Joan and Doris were standing at Mr. Constanza's desk explaining their point.

" It's a story *through ART*." Doris concluded, with Joan standing next to her.

"Okay, all right, good, exxxcellent." Mr. Constanza nodded. Joan noticed he emphasized "excellent" with a drawn-out tone that made it sound sarcastic. She never asked but hoped this was because he was a fan of The Simpsons TV show. She snapped back to the present as he continued, "This will be a 4-credit course applied toward any advanced placement."

:::

That was five weeks ago, and now, coasting down the other side of Heart Attack Hill, Doris spotted her dad with a hose in hand, spraying a metal project. They exchanged waves, and Doris continued towards Pa and Gram's shed.

"Heyyy," Doris called out as she approached the shed where Pa had Pony up on a stand. He was still hunched over, working on the engine with a long-handled tool. Doris watched in amazement as Pa and Joan seemed to work intuitively together. When needed, Joan had the next tool ready, or Pa would hand her something and she'd be prepared to take it. Joan was on the other side of the motorcycle, ready to assist.

"How's the patient?" Doris asked, standing next to Pa, still unable to comprehend the technicalities of what he was doing. She looked at Joan, who shrugged.

"It's a good day," Pa said

"You got it!" Joan smiled at Doris, who responded motionless, raising her eyebrows. "He unfroze a bolt; it's one that we'd have to ask your dad to make if we didn't get it or order it from somewhere. It could have been a nightmare." Doris nodded but didn't fully understand and snapped a photo of the progress. "Oh, great idea," Joan said, pulling out her camera and choosing a close-up shot of the bolt lying on its side in the palm of Pa's hand. "So now we can rebuild the carburetor, and that gets us close. Right, Pa?" He nodded. "Kadence should bring the new wheels and tires by today or tomorrow. We're getting close!" Joan said with enthusiasm, looking at Pa and then turning to Doris. "How was practice?"

"I nailed the reverse 1 1/2 tuck. It'll be in our next meet. I'm a little nervous; the coach wants me to take it up to the three-meter and do it as a reverse layout. I'm freaking out when I think about it, but I fight that with Michael Jordan in my head saying, 'Being nervous isn't bad. It just means something important is happening.'"

"I like that one." Joan nodded.

Pa pointed at a small wrench-like tool, and Joan handed it to him.

"What's that dives 'DD'?" Joan asked. She knew that the degrees of difficulty were computed into the scores.

"On 1 meter, it's a 2, or maybe it's 2.1, I forget. But when I lay it out it'll be 2.6." Doris' voice drifted off in thought as she watched hands and metal working together before her, "2.6 would be nice and it would be prettier with a half twist." Doris sighed following her attention that was drawn to the sound of a plane she watched pass above.

"2.6? Wow, that's high, right?!" Joan asked, following Doris' gaze to the plane flying overhead.

"Yeah, maybe I'll be making contrails." Doris joked as Pa laughed. Joan and Doris exchanged surprised glances at Pa's reaction; even surprised that he was listening. They laughed and shrugged at each other over Pa.

"Not everything has to be competitive, Do." Pa began, his voice lighthearted as he made Doris' name sound like a sound. He was squinting and using the special metric tool before handing it up to Joan who then put it back where she had found it. Pa pushed himself up from the concrete floor, pulling on Pony's foot peg above him for a little help.

"What do you mean, Pa?" Doris asked.

"In school, we have tests, and tests show us where we are in our studies, our progress, right?" Both the girls nodded. Pa was wiping his hands on an already dirty cloth he had grabbed from a nail on the shed's wall. "Tests outside of school do that too, understand?" The girls shook their heads no. "Fear'n the unknown isn't helping you or anyone, or any situation." He paused. "But celebrating it does." He saw both girls stunned with their eyebrows up, looking at him. "You do your personal best, forget the rest," he said with a squeak from his cheek and a nod and knelt draping himself over Pony again doing something Doris hadn't a clue, but Joan was watching carefully.

"I just don't know. When I'm standing at the edge of the board and looking down, it still looks and feels like a mile to the water. My knees shake. I'm not sure I can do better. This might be my best." Doris said, her voice filled with a tone of vulnerable uncertainty.

Pa looked up at Doris; picked a tiny thing from Joan's cupped hand and crouched back over announcing, "Never let the fear of striking out get in your way. Babe Ruth."

"Who's that?" Joan asked.

"Yeah?" Doris added.

Pa groaned. "Really? Babe Ruth? Look it up." Joan had been hearing this instruction a lot this past month, usually regarding motorcycle parts or functions. Both girls laughed.

"So, what's this or that called you're working on, Doctors?" Doris asked, plopping down and beginning some light leg stretches seated on the ground. She listened to Joan explain, with Pa correcting when needed. Doris tried to stay engaged and interested, but she had given up mentally and lost track of the technical details last week when they both explained over and over the beauty of dual, single or something carburetors

MOM

"…and motorcycle companies have designers just like the clothing business." Joan knew Doris was aware of this because she watched TV and movies and was online a lot at night. These industries have their own designers and their own shows, and she would often mention a TV show called Project Runway that featured fashion designers. "It's like a fashion show but about motorcycles; back in 1972, which I think is my favorite historical year, Norton Motorcycles hired an engineer; a guy who worked for Rolls Royce, to design a motorcycle and that design won all sorts of design awards around the world."

As Joan spoke, Gram walked by her door and waved hello. Joan and Doris replied simultaneously, "Hi," and waved back. Doris checked her cell phone and added, "I need to go, Jo. See ya!" She walked out of Joan's room and down the hall. Glancing over her shoulder at Gram, she gave a loud "Byeeee" and headed out the door to get home by dinnertime.

Joan's call with her mom was scheduled for later that night. Joan's mom had texted her the news earlier in the day. Normally, her mom would call from a private communication room set up on-site, a sort of box for private phone calls. But today she was in a larger tent, and it was fun to see other people walking around in the background behind her mom as they talked.

Joan watched Gram walk away far enough not to hear, then turned back to the screen and leaned in with a smile.

"Joan?" Mom asked, smiling with raised eyebrows.

"I think I'm better, all better, Mom. I hardly have them at all anymore. Once, when Pa revved up the engine, I thought it was one starting, but it didn't go anywhere." Joan said, her smile beaming through the laptop screen. Her mom was so beautiful, even through Zoom. She had her hair up and was wearing her stethoscope which meant to Joan that she was either on duty or had just finished her shift. Her mom was a superhero in Joan's eyes. Her mom's light brown eyes matched her khakis and Joan thought she could easily have a boyfriend if she wanted to, but she didn't push it. As her mom had told her once before, "I'll let you know when I'm ready."

"And still no headaches?" her mom inquired.

Joan shook her head, still smiling.

"And Saturn?" her mom asked, her expression growing more serious.

"No pain, no heat. Nothin'!" Joan exclaimed, raising a thumbs-up. "I think I'm better."

Joan watched her knowing her mom was analyzing the situation. Her mom always had an expressionless face and eyes that didn't blink; they looked like those of a robot, and her head would perform little nods as if agreements to conversations were happening inside her. After a couple of moments of silence, Joan's mom shrugged, took a deep breath and her face lit up with one big smile.

"Okay, Joan. That's over a month now. Oh, honey this is great news. It's time to celebrate!"

"Yeah, when you come home, we'll celebr-," Joan was interrupted by her mom's transformation into 'the look'.

"Oh, no. Mom, nooooo!" Joan pleaded, rolling her eyes. She knew her mom was in what is called the 'media tent' not alone but surrounded by a row of computers with other people nearby. Joan cringed.

Since the attack eight years ago they have celebrated every victory no matter how large or small. It was a positive moment, a way to rise above their grief, pain, or physical injuries. They made a pact that since they couldn't change what had happened, they would change the way they reacted to those events. They had each other and decided on the happiest song they could think of, one they both loved, to use as their anthem. Pharrell Williams' 'Happy'.

Her mom laughed, "Oh, yeah, here we go!" She got up and tilted the computer so Joan could see her dancing behind her chair. Then Joan could hear the music intro backing her mom up for the full dramatic effect.

"What? What did you do?" Joan's voice was a mixture of laughter and shock. "I hear that!"

They both laughed and leaned towards their screens, towards each other. Joan's mom bobbed her head with the music.

"I had a feeling this day would come, girl! Let's go now, let's blow it up our style... up!"

Joan surrendered, rolling her eyes as she swayed her head side to side with the beat. It was amazing how admittedly badly they both sang but she joined in anyway. Nope, no singing talent in this family, Joan thought as she got up moving her laptop from where it lay on the bed up onto the desk so she could stand in front of it.

Her mom was smiling ear to ear, clapping. She didn't seem to mind the attention from her colleagues, and even a couple of people behind her mom in the background were clapping along as she let herself go and sang along thousands of miles away:

> *"It might seem crazy what I'm 'bout to say*
> *Sunshine she's here, you can take a break*
> *I'm a hot air balloon that could go to space*
> *With the air, like I don't care, baby, by the way*
>
> *(Because I'm happy)*
> *Clap along if you feel like a room without a roof*
> *(Because I'm happy)*
> *Clap along if you feel like happiness is the truth*
> *(Because I'm happy)*
> *Clap along if you know what happiness is to you*
> *(Because I'm happy)*
> *Clap along if you feel like that's what you wanna do ....."*

FIRST BREATH

"Turn that off for a bit will ya, Joan?"

"Sheesh, good idea, Pa." Joan scooped herself up from lying on her back against the cool concrete. The two of them had been down there a long time these past couple of days hooking up the electrics from underneath Pony. Usually, the radio was a companion to them bridging their generation gap when it felt like a crevasse. It was blabbing on again about corruption this and that.

Kadence had dropped off a small envelope with wiring Pa had Joan found online and ordered earlier that week. It was a struggle for Pa's large fingers to reach through Pony's smaller intricate areas, but he didn't lose his patience and Joan's hands waited for any requests for help. Joan stretched her arms up high, and she looked out spotting Kadence's truck way over there.

Early on, when Kadence frequently stopped with many small packages, he suddenly stopped his usual fluent movement one day. He stared at Joan so intently it scared her a little and he winked. "I know yer new around here and it's none of m'business but I need to report if Pa has lost it and y'all are fixin' to build a nuclear bomb." He smiled as he passed Joan with a long box and walked to Pa's shed. Joan followed, surprised and smiling. Since she had first met him, Kadence was always in such a rush; with a few runs of sweat from his forehead and a job she thought seemed adventurous but the pace unfriendly. However, Kadence was like everyone else she was learning; they all seemed to feel at home with Pa and Gram. It was like everyone in town was as close as family or something.

Sometimes Gram would run into Kadence in town while she was on errands, and he'd hand her a package to bring home for Pa. But for the most part, Kadence stopped several times a week and he hadn't popped out to see the progress since it started. He'd ask Joan if all was well. He knew that if Gram called Joan's name when his truck stopped, she had some treat; cookies, maybe a slice of pie to deliver to him. Then Joan would dash first to Gram and then to the truck, holding something out to Kadence when he'd appear from the back of his truck with whatever had come to help Pony heal.

Deliveries were like Christmas mornings; an exchange of surprise gifts. Both Joan and Kadence would open their gifts or recognize what they were and say aloud to one another what they got while smiling. "Oh, the gaskets are here!" and "Mmm, Brownies!" It was fun; and although it was understood by all that Kadence was in a hurry for a living, throughout these past two months, Joan had learned that Kadence has two dogs named Homer and Simpson. He enjoys pickleball and traveling. He not only sees their mail carrier Blaise but has gone fishing at the river with her. In New York, Joan had never even seen the delivery people who dropped things off at her building.

"It's like the radio sucks us into some vortex with the music and the next thing we know we are listening to the news which is fine really until it becomes all about," Joan made air quotes and lowered her voice into a demonic tone, "the name that shall not be mentioned." She swiped her right hand across her jeans and tuned the radio to the other station she knew Pa liked, "91.9 KPTZ, eclectic authentic radio." they would say every hour. She knew his favorite was Lizzz with three z's and her program called 'Musical Chairs'. "She spins on a razor's edge" he would say while tuning in.

"Better?" Joan called over.

"Better than listening to that giant orange basketball talk his ignorance." she heard him say in a tone loaded with sarcasm. Joan took a sip of the lemonade Gram had brought out to them a while back. It was warm now but still refreshing. She broke off a piece of Gram's fudge and quickly downed the rest of her lemonade, popped the fudge in her mouth and brought over Pa's half glass of lemonade and a piece of fudge for him. The radio was playing a song and she had heard Pa singing a few words along with her. She interrupted him saying, "Here." Joan was sitting next to Pa and Pony.

Pa groaned and sat up, "Great idea."

Joan and Pa had a similar pace to the day. He orchestrated it and Joan fell into its comfort. She liked it here a lot and then thought it must have been the thousandth time she had said that to herself.

"Ah." Pa handed the empty glass back to Joan. Wiping his brow with the back of his forearm he added, "Thanks." And he popped the piece of fudge in his mouth. "Your Gram makes the best lemonade this side of the Milky Way." He leaned down again.

"Yeah, she's amazing, Pa. How did you two meet?"

Joan learned to be patient after asking a question. There was no need to rush anything here, especially conversation with Pa. He had a lot of it in him and it would come if she allowed space. Joan watched Pa wince as he tried to push two tiny electrical connectors together before he replied, "Even a blind squirrel gets a nut once in a while."

"Heyyy." Joan heard Doris riding up. Joan and Pa knew they had been at it for hours since lunch when they heard Doris ride up each day.

"Hi, Dodo! How'd it go?" It was Joan's regular greeting now.

Doris leaned her bike against the shed and walked over to Pa and Joan. It was a much slower, quieter setting than the town where she came from.

"Rocky wanted me to give you this. He said it was yours but needed a part of some sort." Doris explained.

Pa replied as usual and without looking up, "All righty, thank you Dodo. If you would please, put it on my bench in the shop there." He was still struggling to push the two connectors together. "How are you doing today?"

"Ooo- Do, Gram made fudge. Have some, there by the radio!" Joan interrupted.

Doris noticed the bench was now much cleaner than it had been all week. She placed the handheld vacuum on the workbench, walked over to the portable radio, fine-tuned it, and grabbed a piece of Gram's fudge.

"Mmm, Gawowwd I love her fudge!" Doris exclaimed while tuning in the radio better.

"Well, that's much clearer, thanks," Joan called out to Doris, just now noticing the radio tuning with relief.

Pa groaned and rose to a sitting position. He stood up, stretched his limbs, rotated his wrists and neck and then took a deep breath and let out a little belch that said lemonade and fudge. He said, "Okay, let's check electrical," as he walked over for a piece of fudge then behind Pony.

"Brakes," Pa said.

Joan reached and squeezed the handlebar lever. Then, the foot brake. "Great job, Pa! See Doris? This brake is on this side, they put the foot brake below here on the other side.

"Good," Pa confirmed, and he walked to his workbench, plopped down the tools he had picked up off the ground when he got up, then looked at the vacuum. He walked back, taking a detour in his gait to grab another piece of fudge.

"Why isn't that up at the handlebar like the other?" Doris asked Joan.

"Because that's the throttle, the gas pedal on a motorcycle. It's safer this way," Joan explained. Doris asked a lot of questions and Joan loved answering them; it tested her on what she'd been learning online along with what Pa had been teaching her. Joan felt comfortable in discovering how things are made and why. She felt ready for Pony but knew it was completely up to Pa.

"Okay, ignition," Pa said, wiping his fingertips on his pants.

"Really? We haven't started her yet with the ignition. Wow, big moment." Joan looked at them both smiling snapping her head from Pa to Doris and back to Pa as he turned the key to "ON" and pushed the ignition. The high-pitched grind churned again and again, and then Pony started up.

"Saving knees all over the world," Pa quietly said to himself as he unbuckled his knee pads and handed them to Joan to put away with the direction of his nod and a point. He stretched his arms high in the air, turned and twisted, stretching his low back and took a deep breath. "All right, good, she's got lungs, cut it."

Joan promptly turned off the ignition switch and looked at Doris with raised eyebrows. Doris returned the same look and asked, "So does that mean you, uhm, *we* did it? You're finished? Pony is healed?" They both looked at Pa.

Gram had heard the engine from the house where she was washing the lettuce she'd just brought in from the garden. She saw Joan and Doris jumping up and down with their hands in the air and holding each other, then Pa, and finally, the three of them arm in arm next to Pony. Gram went into her bedroom and brought out the large square box Kadence had delivered weeks ago, then walked to the shed.

"DORIS!" Gram called out. Doris ran to her. "You'll want to video this. Do you have your phone with you?" she said quietly to Doris at her side as they walked up to Pony, shining, all in one piece, erected up on the center stand.

JANE

"There." Joan pointed.

"I saw that too, a long one," Doris added.

They were lying on their backs on Doris' porch roof watching the stars. Gram had mentioned it was time for the Perseids meteor shower and the clear night was perfect for celebrating.

The two of them had brought up blankets and popcorn. Gram had also sent Joan over with a thermos of hot chocolate.

"So, can you ride Pony to my meet?"

"Well, I guess so. I can take the county road over to Martha's Landing and then cut across the Bertino Owl Trail to the County Pool, right? Yeah, I'm allowed to ride on county roads and a few city streets when necessary, with my permit, so yeah, I think so. That'll be fun."

"Oh! Did you see that one? It had a tail?! I think Pa's rubbed off on you some, the way you said, 'I think so' sounded just like him."

"He's the best," Joan said.

"I have the permit; the riding clothes and Gram's helmet fits great. Mom says I should go for it, and Pa says he'll teach me in the morning. So great, eh?"

They both lay on their backs in silence.

Joan asked, "Are you scared?"

Doris said, "Yeah, still. I nailed it in practice the last couple of days, but it's scary up there. The three-meter board scares the fun out of it, I guess."

"OO~ooo," they said in unison as a star shot across the sky.

"You scared?" Doris asked.

"Yeah, kinda now that Pony is healed up. It's like I'm healed up too. I don't know what to do next. I get a little nervous when I think about it for a long time."

"Yeah. Michael Jordan said, 'Never say never, because limits, like fears, are often just illusions.'"

"Yeah." They both repeated slowly at the same time while gazing up. They laughed.

The next morning Joan had started oatmeal for the three of them and was getting the large bag of blueberries she and Gram had picked together out of the freezer when Gram came around the corner of the kitchen.

"Good morning, Joan, Joanie, Jo-Jo, my Joan of Arc" she added a moment later, "Joanie baloney" and she went to prepare coffee but hugged Joan instead as she noted it was already on the maker. She knew Joan must be jumping with excitement, but on the outside, she was playing it really cool. Gram gifted her the top-of-the-line Arai brand helmet the previous day to test ride the old motorcycle with Pa. She had Googled reviews and had come across a Jay Leno interview with an Arai representative online. They talked in the video for 40 minutes about helmets and covered everything from fit to specs. She knew she was buying the best and took Joan's head measurements one day telling her she would be knitting a fall hat only to fool her into hopefully buying her the correct fitting helmet. And she had; snug and to Gram's satisfaction. Joan would not be going fast, she knew that considering this County, but when it came to a helmet, she would not allow anything less than the best.

"So?" Gram took Joan by the shoulders. "Today is your day. I realize that, and I want you to know that although I am not a fan of motorcycles, as you well know, I have FULL confidence in your ability to take what you have book-learned and put it to use on the road."

Joan just couldn't hold it in. "Gram, I promise I'll be more than careful. I am so excited to ride Pa's Pony!"

Gram shook Joan's shoulders and smiled. "I trust you and I am so happy you are happy, my Joan!"

Gram nodded into Joan's eyes, "I want you to know that I VALUE your intelligence and your CHOICES, and I trust you will be careful." It seemed important somehow for Gram to emphasize her words, to somehow wake up a new level of compassion and care in Joan.

Joan started to tear up, but just then heard Pa's boots on the wooden floor walking their way. She smiled, hugged Gram quickly and turned back to attend to the oatmeal. "Good morning Pa!" Joan called out, shaking her tears back. "Oatmeal with blueberries this morning 'sound good? Coffee is on and your Earl Grey is brewing!"

"Mm, good morning, ladies. There are only two kinds of tea, Earl and Grey," Joan chimed in with him on the often recited, "and Grey," and Gram laughed.

It had been about an hour of slow, quiet advice and a lot of polite listening, needing the stamina of Joan's concentration, and then the three of them were outside. Gram watched from the kitchen door's stoop as the two walked Pony around to the front of the house's driveway. Joan heard a whistle and figured that it was Doris telling her dad she was heading their way.

Sure enough, a moment later she was running over and already holding her phone up, obviously videoing the big moment. Joan waved.

Doris walked up and propped the phone up in the crook of a branch of the rhododendron above them for a good overshot.

Pa had Joan on the seat with him the day before. He sat behind her and had his hands atop hers, guiding her through the smooth motions of shifting into first gear and slowly releasing the clutch. Pa was impressed by how quickly she grasped the coordination and order of shifting both up and downshifting. He noticed her execution was clean and confident, and she was right; it did fit her well.

He bent down and looked into her eyes before continuing, "Two important things. YOU come first, not Pony. Never try to save Pony. People fall, whether it be in a ditch, sand, gravel, or this here driveway. I'm not saying YOU will, but if you do, walk away. Do not try to save the bike. Got it?"

Joan nodded with seriousness.

"And this will be more difficult to remember as you get more comfortable, but it is actually more important to remember the more comfortable you get."

"They don't see me."

"That's right," Pa said, surprised that Joan said that. "That's exactly what I want to get through to you."

"I read that all over the online safety sites, Pa."

"That makes me a happy mother duckling. You are invisible. Be invisible, Joan. We ride as if we are invisible to all cars, well everything really. Do this, and you'll be safe."

"Yes, I will, I promise."

"Well, alright then, I trust you. Remember what you've read and what I have said. You have your phone on you?" Joan nodded. "Okay, do me the honors." Pa smiled into her eyes with a nod.

"Oh PA!" Joan couldn't hold back her tears; she stepped into his body and hugged Pa tight, holding on longer than usual. Pa cleared his throat and glanced at Gram, which Gram knew as a signal that he was feeling emotional. Gram felt the heat of tears welling up in her own eyes. Doris was standing with her phone held out in front of her, happily recording video.

Joan looked at Pony, the stand it leaned on, and deliberately threw Saturn over Pony. She felt the comfort of the bike between her thighs before she had even gone on a ride. She loved Pa's Pony. "Okay, ready?" She looked at Pa, Gram, and Doris, and started to cry.

She started to put her new pearl white helmet on and paused, sitting on the bike and giggled. "I can't go anywhere with my eyes all foggy like this!" She laughed. She pushed the snug helmet down on her head, flipped up its visor and reaching through gave it a pull and jiggle until it was comfortable. She wiped her eyes and flipped down the dark visor, thankful that the three of them couldn't see that she was crying still. The smell of the helmet within was a mixture of leather, hot plastic, and her own breath. She felt so isolated even though she was still in the driveway, the three of them looking at each other, smiling and waiting for Joan to take off. Joan knew the only challenge she hadn't practiced was braking with her prosthetic, but while on the bike the day before with Pa she only needed to push her body forward and to the right for enough pressure downward on the brake pedal. Combined with the handbrake she didn't see any problems. Pony's engine died and it was the perfect release for everyone to laugh out loud. Joan clapped her hands and started Pony up again, popped into first gear, and slowly drove the curve of the dirt driveway out onto the road.

Pa was standing between Doris and Ma as Joan rode off. He reached his long arms across the backs of each of them and rested his hands on the shoulders of each. He gave them both a squeeze into him. "All right, okay, are we all a mess?" Pa was standing between Doris and Ma as Joan rode off, the three of them had tears in their eyes. Doris nodded. Ma nodded and sniffed, "Berry pie sound good?"

Joan felt the heat and weight of the helmet in the summer sun and for a moment thought she might be triggered by the claustrophobic feelings she was experiencing in the helmet, but clearly thought to flip up its visor and felt relief. No trigger. She decided not to ride the familiar way to town but rather turn right, up over the rise, and down to the river where she and Doris swam last Saturday. She knew there were a few intersections along the way where she could practice her starts and stops, wanting to achieve a smoother transition between gears. She wanted to impress herself, and Pa of course. She knew Pa would notice the improvement when he saw her ride up the drive on her return along with the confidence she felt. Just on the other side of the last rise in the road, Joan pulled Pony over to the side of the road and put the kickstand down. She noted that she hadn't stopped smiling. She took a deep breath, unbuckled her full-faced helmet and slid it slowly up and off her head, holding onto it. She dismounted and stood next to Pony. Just the two of them and the sound of the breeze as she walked around looking at Pony. They were alone. Free. Joan felt like this once before. She remembered it was when she left the hospital after months of surgeries and therapy. They released her, and it felt like anything was possible.

When Joan was in the hospital she had a favorite nurse, Jane. Jane seemed to always be on duty when Joan was hurting the most. To Joan, Jane was magical. After Joan awoke from surgery of some kind she would see Jane, either next to her or just walking in as she woke up. Jane had eyes as blue as the sky, and she talked to Joan with an adult voice, not talking down to her as if she were a baby. It was like Jane knew Joan was an adult just waiting to grow up and Joan respected her. Jane always seemed to say something that indicated she understood Joan or her take on things happening to her.

There was something Jane said the day Joan left the hospital that seemed to apply to this moment with Pony as Pony left her own hospital shed.

"Well, Pony," recalling Jane's wise words, Joan was slowly, carefully remembering to say the words correctly. "Today is the day you get to expect the unexpected and seek what waits to be found."

She sat on Pony and waited until she felt inspired to move. She wanted Pony to have a say in where they would go and when they would go. It was Pony's day as well after all. "Hey, Happy Birthday Pony!" Joan said and patted the cool gas tank in front of her. "Happy Birthday!" she shouted aloud inside her helmet and enjoyed the echoey, muffled effect within. They started up and smoothly clicked into first gear; a little bouncy start eased into second, a bit smoother, now third aimed for the river up ahead.

When Joan downshifted from third to second, she felt a little shake that rumbled, more of a flutter than the previous downshift and made a mental note to ask Pa about it. She knew to take it slow, "Parts need patience to break in." She remembered the wisdom. "Lubrication, warmth, and time to smooth out tiny imperfections within the metal-on-metal relationships." Kind of like people meeting new people; Joan just now realized this thought. She liked thinking while she rode like this. She felt that the combination of movement forward and the space around allowed for her thoughts to do the same. She felt the warmth of the engine on the insides of her legs and leaned down now and then for a whiff of Pony's engine. It was a steep road approaching the river. Joan braked quite a bit, noting slow was more enjoyable than going fast. She could feel that her rear brake could use a slight adjustment. Joan loved feeling Pony's weight as they leaned into a corner here and then the next one, noting she needed to work on her comfort leaning left as she was more confident leaning right. Yes, she thought, curves are the funnest. She would seek out some curvy roads to ride in the future.

Joan downshifted to first on the paved road dusted with gravel and then quickly a mix of gravel on the pavement as Pony slowed to a stop. Joan didn't want to kick up any gravel into Pony's underbelly and this was close enough to the riverside. Joan could see handmade signs, one at the boat ramp and another at the river's edge where they had watched kayakers enter the water, "The Put-in." Doris taught her last Saturday. One of the signs read "No Pipeline," Another read "You Can't Drink Oil, Keep It In The Soil." There was a small camper van parked parallel to the river and a tall, large, converted cargo van with two kayaks on the top in a rack. It was open in the back, and it looked like someone had been camping inside.

Joan was intoxicated by the smell of Pony's warm engine. She walked Pony up a few more feet on the right side of the gravel parking lot, under the shade of a flowering Dogwood tree in the midst of turning its flowers dusty pink. Pony looked stunning under her, and Joan took a photo of the two of them together and sent it to Gram and Doris. She would have also included Pa, but he has yet to surrender to this 21st century of owning a cell phone, or a computer. Joan included in the text, "At the river. Pony has been perfect. We are taking a break." Joan added a motorcycle emoji, a horse emoji, a water emoji, a red heart emoji and a smiley emoji. She wanted to update them even though it had been less than a half hour. She hadn't been away from one of them that long, and experience had shown that it's best if she initiates the text rather than wait for others to keep in touch as everyone wasn't so sure about her comfort, even though she was. Her phone immediately rang back, a text from Doris: "Great photo, what a beauty! Happy maiden voyage to you both! Gram, Pa, and I haven't moved yet. Hangin' here in the drive waving goodbye, Haha"

Joan could feel the connection she had between herself and Pony. As she walked away from Pony, she felt herself not wanting to be too far away. She walked back to Pony, placed the helmet at the foot of the bike as she was taught, and peeled off the small red and black Kevlar jacket Gram found for her at Feron's in town. It was a size too big, but both Gram and Joan agreed on cooler days it would allow for a light sweater underneath. The pile atop Pony's seat now spoke to her; she would need saddlebags if she was to travel anywhere. She shook out her long, brown-haired ponytail, rubbed her eyes, and walked to the water's edge. Joan removed her boots and socks now and thought to just stand in the water and feel the river move. It was a day of moving forward, she thought. She closed her eyes and listened to the river, then turned and looked back at Pony, as if to transfer this baptismal feeling.

"'Ello there." A youngish woman waved as she walked towards Joan and the parking lot. Joan hadn't noticed there was a person standing in the river just up from her until then. She appeared to be alone. She had a long, thick, blonde braid reflecting the sun and it hung below her waist to one side in front of her. She wore rolled-up jeans and a big loose-knit sweater. She seemed older than Joan's mom but younger than her Gram and she was walking towards Joan slowly in the water, but with ease, not in an unsure, awkward way, careful not to slip on the rocks below as Joan did. "'Ope I didn't scare you?" the woman smiled with a smile that seemed to sparkle like her hair.

ANNABELLE

Joan looked around, not sure if the woman was talking to her. She glanced over both shoulders, then over to Pony, then back to the young woman standing out in the water.

"Oh, hi there, good morning!" Joan waved her hand quickly up and down, feeling a bit shy. The woman stopped a few feet from Joan, standing still with her eyes closed, chin lifted upward, and shoulders relaxed. She then opened her eyes, reached down, and Joan watched her feel around for something under the water. In her hands, up came a large boulder about the size of her head, and then she walked toward the mouth of the river. After holding it to her chest for what seemed to Joan like a long hug she placed it down gently.

Joan sat at the water's edge, curiously watching the woman, sensing that something more was going on here than a woman playing with rocks. She anchored her heels in the pebbly sandy shoreline, wiggled her butt into a comfortable position, and continued to watch this woman. The woman seemed fine with Joan observing. Now and then, the woman would look up at Joan and smile. It feels like a ceremony, Joan thought.

Ma and Pa lived on the edge of reservation land and had plenty of Indigenous friends and their friends over for lunch on their way to the river. In danger of a gas and oil company laying a pipeline through and along its fragile ecosystem, people had been coming and going to protest. Ma had said this had been going on for years now. Some stayed for long periods of time, protecting the river and watching over its shoreline, on the lookout for sneaky construction intruders coming through without the permission of the people of their land. There were signs with phone numbers asking people to report any sightings of such actions. When there were signs of activity, the nearby residents spread the word to gain attention for protection. Gram had said, "So far, so good."

Joan's gaze shifted to the opposite end of the river's edge from the open camper, which she assumed was the woman's, and examined the large van. Beach towels were drying atop a kayak on the roof rack and there was a stack of firewood and kindling next to a fire pit with a couple of folding chairs and a cooler. It was evident they were comfortable and had been here longer than just last night.

Joan was lost in thought; her eyes fixed on a small eddy in the water in front of her when the woman approached from upriver onshore.

"Thanks for your help!" The woman smiled.

"Oh, hello again." Joan was surprised and then noticed that she didn't have her usual nervous jump, her personal orange alert asking herself if she was safe before interacting with someone new. She smiled at that and took a deep breath.

"I felt so calm watching whatever you were doing with the rocks there. It seemed like a ceremony of some kind. I hope I didn't intrude if it was one." Joan apologized politely, realizing now that maybe the woman didn't want to talk about it. It was early, and it was a quiet time away from people. Gram had told her this river was considered sacred to many.

"Yes, I'm a sound healer." The woman replied, her voice soft. Joan raised her eyebrows, and the woman continued, "I travel 'round and help wounded waters heal. Rivers, oceans, creeks, lagoons, natural ponds."

"Wow, I've never heard of that. So, you healed the river here? How nice of you." Joan nodded.

" 'know it sounds pretty strange, that's for sure. I'm Annabelle, friends call me Belle for short."

"I'm Joan, Hi." There was silence. The woman bent side to side, stretched her body a bit, and walked out of the water barefoot. Joan asked, "Does the river talk to you and tell you it's sick?"

"'-at's a good way of saying it. Or maybe I listen to it and tune it. I learned from my Uncle Howard. He could make rivers sing; he called it 'tuning.' He'd move large rocks with his powerful arms. One maybe a foot to the left and upstream a yard, and then maybe another behind or turn it over. Or maybe pick up another and place it in the middle of the river, watching the water split and flow down each side of it."

"Like you were doing just now?"

"'Cept I'm not as good as Uncle Howard."

Joan realized that it was a Canadian accent she was hearing. She wasn't sure if it was Canadian or Irish, but the way the woman pronounced "my uncle" had a sort of "OH" sound. It was a sound she had heard from people in town when they said the word "about"; it sounded more like "Ah-bow-t." She was thinking this when Belle continued:

"He could really feel water sources calling out to him from around the globe and he'd go and course-correct their flow. Watching him was like watching a dance. After a while, I could begin to see the energy he'd release in the river, feel its flow better."

"See the energy?"

"Mmm *see* as in sense, feel, eh? Think of the river as you think of your body. It has emotions, a purpose, an environment, systems that affect its health."

"Okay, yeah, that makes sense. It is alive. So, like the gas pipeline threat hurts the river, and you came to heal it?"

"More like I'm helping the river heal itself. It is under stress, and I *hear* that stress in its flow. It speaks to me in a vibrational rhythm: and when I said 'course correct' earlier, it's more like I guide it, supporting its own healing. I redirect its flow and it sings what it needs to me, like a soothing massage to help the body regulate, relax, feel its balance again, you know, eh?"

"That's so cool." Joan was mesmerized by this woman. "How is it now? Are you done?"

"Well, we'll see how it sounds later today and tonight. I kind of want it to hold the new alignment it needs, in other words, change its dressings or work on some deeper woes it wants to release. 'Ope that made sense?"

Joan nodded yes, although she would need to think more on it. "Hey, Belle, you thanked me for helping, how did I do that?"

"Your energy. We're all energy and when we have an intention our energy goes out toward that intention. So earlier you had the intention of some sort of love for the river. Love in the form of appreciation of the river maybe, or thankfulness, or care for me not slipping. I don't know, but I felt your energy reach out and that helps a lot more than just one person." Belle nodded, sitting next to Joan and drawing hearts and shapes in the sand before them. "Uncle Howard once worked a creek all summer and that fall salmon returned to it. People said it was a miracle, but Uncle Howard taught us the river was just too upset for the salmon to smell their way home."

"That's amazing! Why aren't we all doing this?"

"Well, maybe—I hope—one day we will. It's kind of weird sounding, right?"

"Yeah, one Earth, hurtling through space, and we're on it together. Everything connected. It all sounds strange to most folks, so it will take time for us all to come back to respecting nature again. Everything is connected, everything is everything."

"Everything is everything," Joan said out loud, careful with her words. "That's really something to think about."

"Energy. Everything is made from it, and we're all connected." Belle threw those words out so fast with her accent that Joan nodded before her mind could rewind and repeat them mentally, more slowly to herself.

"WOW, that makes real sense! My Grandpa and I just built that motorcycle." Joan smiled, pointing at Pony. "Her name is Pony. She feels alive to me. While we were fixing her up we joked, saying she was healing, but it did feel this way, and this is our first ride. She feels alive, like I'm with a friend."

"Exactly, Joan. You get it! I'm going to make some lunch. Would you like to join me over here?" Belle pointed over to the small camper.

"Lunch?!" Joan realized time had flown. "I better get back home before my Gram and Grandpa get nervous but thank you so much. How fun to meet you, Belle. Thank you for teaching me all this, uhm, energy stuff!"

"'Ope it wasn't too much, I'm really passionate, and I've been told I sound sometimes forceful when I explain that rivers have a voice, they feel and react to the impact of their environment just like we do and... well...there I go again." Belle shook her head and laughed at herself. Joan joined in her laughter.

"No, it wasn't too much, I don't think. Thank you so much." Joan smiled at Belle. "I really should go through." She began using her socks to remove the sand from between her toes before putting her sock on. "Will you be here long?" she asked, looking at Belle.

Belle just shrugged as she walked back to her camper. "Hope to see you again sometime," Joan called after her, and Belle twirled around and waved. "Thanks, Belle," Joan added as Belle waved above her head without turning around.

Doris was helping hold a metal post of the garden fence steady with Joan while Pa wrapped and stretched more deer-proof fencing that had been slowly disintegrating.

"Everything is everything? That is so cool." Doris responded to Joan's recounting of her river visit. "My dad told me that sometimes in his shop, he has to just allow a piece to be left alone and pick up another piece to work with instead of that last pick because it wasn't speaking to him. I never thought of it as everything is made up of energy and so—"

"Like that," Joan interjected. "I'd like to learn more about that, I think. I just don't get it, if we are all of the same stuff, why would we want to hurt each other? You know? Wars, crimes, polluting the river. It's so sad to think about it."

They all worked together, still and quiet for a bit, each lost in their own thoughts. An Asian dove called out about something in the distance. Pa broke the silence, saying, "That ought to do it, ladies. Thank you kindly." He handed Joan the hammer to carry back to the shed and picked up the roll of fencing.

"Let's get Pony up on the stand now and check out her funny shake. We'll give her underbelly a look-see, make sure she settled well after your ride together this morning."

"Thanks, Pa."

"One last picture, this one with you Pa, to end my art piece for school. Joan had been accepted into the same program as Doris for extra credits. "Doris, will you take a pic of Pa, Pony, and me and then a selfie of all of us please?"

There were no wisecracks from Pa about having his picture taken, which surprised Doris a bit. He looked genuinely pleased in the photo.

"Thanks!" Joan exclaimed.

There was a long silence. Joan watched Pa intently, noting the things he was looking at so she could do the same when needed.

DORIS' WORLD

Joan had been sitting on the lawn hill inside the chain link fence, not far from Pony, parked on the other side of the fence a few feet behind her, for about an hour now. She had brought pretzels, lemonade and a banana, all under Pony's seat. Doris had said this might go on for a few hours because there were kids from all over being checked out by representatives of several teams and schools. Doris had heard a rumor that the Olympic coaching staff had sent someone.

Divers were following one another performing the same preliminary dives. Some were obviously terrible, and from their own facial reactions upon surfacing the diving pool seemed to know it as well. Others, Joan proudly included Doris, were scary good, and this would be, as Doris admitted last night, competitive. After each excellent dive gained high scores from the four judges alongside the pool, Joan would watch Doris looking for her reaction to the scores. Joan hadn't noticed Doris showing any nervousness.

There was an order to the divers, Joan noticed. Some divers stayed in the water at the poolside until called, while some liked to jump out and wipe down with their squeegee towel between dives. Doris was one of the latter, Joan noticed. She was social and popular, something Joan hadn't thought of before. Doris didn't talk much about others when they were together, and Joan didn't know to ask. Nor did she even think about it until now as she watched other kids approach Doris, smile, laugh, and nod their heads. She was far from any social pressure to engage, comfortably enjoying watching her friend in another world. From where she sat, she could hear an occasional loud laugh or applause; otherwise, it was just her, Pony, and the sounds of the Cottonwood trees chiming in the wind.

Over the scratchy-sounding loudspeaker, a woman's voice announced that the preliminary dives had been completed and Doris was the first called up. It looked to Joan like more than half the divers were packing up to go and Joan felt sad for them not qualifying to move on. Joan grabbed the jacket she had placed beside her helmet next to her when she arrived and pulled out of her inside pocket the list of dives Doris had been nervous about. She wanted to shout out some encouragement if needed. There were seven listed, three with stars next to them, which meant Doris had been mentioning that one a lot.

It seemed like all the next dives were fairly similar, scoring high sevens and eights on dives Joan had heard Doris say were easy. When Doris scored all nines on an inward 1 1/2 pike on the three-meter, with a difficulty of 2.6 Joan sat up and paid closer attention than before. Her friend was apparently really, really good at this and she relaxed into the fun of what was happening rather than fearing what could happen.

***

Doris brushed her long bangs off to one side, turning her neck back from checking on her bike which leaned next to Pony out in front of the cafe.

"Do people know how good a diver you are? It's like I know a famous person. You said you were nervous about that reverse, but you nailed it with two 10's!"

"I did my best."

"Yeah, you did!" Joan held her hand up for a high-five, leaning forward and standing halfway out of her side of the booth seat with a big smile. Doris giggled and slapped the high-five. "Yeah," Doris went on, "It was easier when I told myself I was doing my best. Doing it for me, nothing and no one else. Forgetting the rest, like Pa said, I mean yeah, I was still scared up there even though I was looking out and not straight down. But through all that, in the dive, during the scariest part, and the part that demanded my concentration, I still took a moment to feel. And that little moment or whatever, well, it felt like I was flying."

"That's so great Dodo! Sometimes I'm on Pony and we are out there near the river where there are these curves on the newly paved road; it is so smooth I feel kinda that way, like I'm flying into the wind. Mmm." Joan looked out the window at Pony looking back at her.

"Maybe we should be pilots," Doris said.

"Or astronauts?" Joan pointed up.

"Or acrobatic skydivers?" Doris suggested.

JOE

"You do look scary just standing here with a bulletproof vest on and your gun and the truck and uniform and all. I don't get scared very easily though. I'm used to the uniforms, but you sure do stick out here at the river where there is softness everywhere. I don't think camouflage is of much help emotion-wise." Joan remarked.

"That's a funny way of putting it." Joe replied.

"Well, I mean all this stiffness, pointy scary metal and stuff...gun. And then there's-" Joan turned to the water and used her upper body to bounce and flow, showing the opposite.

"Yep, I see what you mean now. I guess when I am in it looking out from this get-up, I don't think about that." Joe turned around and looked at the truck he drove in with Rebecca, his partner, now was lying across the front cab, leaning against the door with the top of her head tilted out the window. She was looking at her phone and would have a quick outburst of a laugh or grumble while looking at her phone. Joan figured it must be a game she was really into.

"Oh, it's quite a contrast!" Joan laughed. She enjoyed Joe, and over the past two weeks of visits she had brought them one of Gram's brownies, a couple of pasties, and shared a few handfuls of Blaise's favorites, salted baked almonds. Joe had taught her some rope knots he thought she might find helpful in life. The trucker's hitch was her favorite, as it could be of so much use rather than just a tricky knot.

Joe's radio went off with some chatter. Sometimes he could talk over it, and sometimes he'd hold up a finger, look serious, and respond, walking away from her for the duration of the call. There were different call sounds before the chatter and one of the sounds reminded her of the fireman. When he was carrying her his radio speaker was above her on his shoulder, making that same sound before each chatter.

Today she asked Joe, "What does that alarm that sometimes comes on before the beep thing mean before the voice when you get a call?"

"There's a different cadence for that situation's status." Joe said quite seriously before adding "They all say one thing to all of us: 'Wake up, pay attention, and serve'."

Joan nodded. "That makes a lot of sense. Thank you." She lowered her head, playing with the sand and rock combination at her feet, then looked up when the wind chimed the leaves of the alder trees. She wasn't sure how long she was lost in her thoughts and memories when Joe said, "You okay in there, Joan?"

"Uh, yeah, thanks, sorry. Hmph. Actually, I'm really great now. I have always wondered what those beeps and horn sounds mean when they squawk over your radios. I was in..." She pointed at her prosthetic, "trouble at the Pentagon bombings. I mean, I was IN it. Ground zero. I don't remember much, just little bits sometimes. I was carried out by a fireman. I'll always remember the sounds and while he was carrying me his radio speaker was on his shoulder like yours and my head was next to it and I kept hearing it go off as he carried me out of there." Joan hadn't shared that with anyone other than her mom a couple of years earlier.

"Oof tha—" Joe said softly, shaking his head. as he wiped away a tear that had made it down his cheek before he caught on.

"Well, now it feels like you know my whole life story." Joan widened her arms and shrugged. Her arms felt lighter, and she realized she felt lighter within herself everywhere. It felt freeing to get all that out. She hadn't done that yet outside of family and Doris.

Joe coughed and sniffed, nodding his head slowly. "You got out, but it's still in there, huh?" Joe asked knowingly.

"Yeah, that's it exactly. Exactly how it feels, Joe. I've never been able to put it in words. I used to have these video playbacks in my head like I was there again, it was real with a bunch of smells and sounds." Joan paused, taking a deep breath. "But they've kinda left, just this summer and now just the feeling is here now. Well, there is the memory of then and the memory of now about then. I think that makes sense?"

Joe, leaning against the pickup, shifted his posture then leaned back again. "I do believe you are doing just fine. *Can't never could.* You've got all kinds of gumption in your britches, climbing out of you. Lil' piece of advice?"

Joan guessed he was offering, not asking her for advice. His Mississippi could be confusing, she noted. "Oh, yes, please."

"I keep a journal. Do you keep a journal?"

"Nah-uh." Joan was feeling the new lightness within her.

"I spend a lot of time alone, as you can see here." They both smiled looking back at Rebecca, who was still smiling at her phone. "Writing stuff down is like going into a time machine. I can go back and figure things out or imagine my future and say what I want to see happen. See?" Joan nodded. "But the advice here? Well, I think it'd be good for you to write down what happens to you in everyday life each day. It kind of helps make time more solid and doesn't let it get all muddy and flow by. Helps keep the muggy past clear from seeping in the way of today, tomorrow's memory of today. Does that make sense?"

"I think so. I mean, sometimes it feels like the past couple of months have just run into the same if it weren't for coming here and seeing what's new or who's new. Meeting you. Like that?"

"Yep. It can all just flow behind us if we want it to, or we can capture moments that are important. For instance, I am looking forward to tonight writing about my day here with you and what I've learned."

"Wow, you've learned from me?" Joan was surprised.

"Joan, you've taught me or maybe I should say that you've introduced me to deeper layers within and fresh perspectives of courage, grace, and inner strength inside myself. Thank you for that."

"I see what you mean now. Aw, thanks, cool." Joan nodded her head, smiling.

"Cool? Well, groovy, girl!" Joe kidded.

"Hey, I say 'cool.' I like it." She defended his sarcasm. "You're cool."

"Okay, okay, Joan. Heh heh. You're a 'trip.'"

While riding home on Pony, Joan recalled her mom suggesting she keep a diary years ago when she was a patient. Her mom said it would help her stay focused on her progress and goals in physical therapy. She did try a few times. Each time she'd write a bit, maybe a page or so, then later tear it out, thinking she wouldn't want someone finding it and reading her thoughts. Could she do it again? Was it different now? Did she really care what others thought? She was lost in thought about her regarding what others thought of her. Thoughts about whether this was what people typically wrote in their diaries continued until she approached a pile of rock and concrete on the side of the road. She slowed down, downshifted into second gear and proceeded cautiously. She had learned on previous rides that some feral cats lived in that area, and one might run onto the highway. Pony, back up to speed now, was purring contentedly. She seemed as happy to be in the wind as Joan was herself, Joan thought.

Doris arrived at the driveway just minutes after she had parked Pony, and Joan had unpacked the Ziplock bag she and Gram had been reusing so much on rides with Pony that it had become a game between them to see how long this one bag could last. Joan blew into it, turned the bag upside down to dump the crumbs out and noticed no pits, tears, or holes. It was still in good condition, ready for another use.

"How's Joe and Rebecca?" Doris asked, flipping her head to sweep her bangs up and to the side.

"That was a blast today. I gave Joe the 10-36 on 9/11."

"The 10-36 Joan, you're a sponge."

"How was practice?" Joan asked, grabbing the empty thermos with her free hand and the two of them began walking toward Gram's kitchen.

"Alright. I guess. Yeah, I'm good. I'm still working on nailing my full twisting 1 1/2 layout on the three-meter. There's no hiding in that dive. It needs to be seamless. Coach says it is the emotional sale that will speak for me. To rip the entry isn't just the usual hands and water line up, it is a total body balance that starts back with my hurdle -the intentions I begin my hurdle with. Intention is everything. The driver of the diver Coach says. He thinks TeamUSA wants me, but thinking isn't enough. He said they need to be sold on me and 80% of sales is emotion."

"That sounds confusing! The dive and Coach. Joan shook her head.

"Yeah, and if it gets in my head too much it can haunt me then, you know, SPLAT. So, I listen to Coach when he says all I have to do is my part and he'll do his, which is much easier for me to understand. Otherwise, SPLAT.

"Ouch," Joan winced.

"Uh-huh. I don't want to think about the people parts; I'll leave that up to the Coach. That's why he's my Coach, and I'll concentrate on the SPLATS!" Doris emphasized 'splat' again, knowing it made Joan cringe. Doris caught the door behind Joan before it could slap back on her and walked in. "Hi, Gram! Hi Pa! Caught you at teatime?" Doris opened the fridge and grabbed a root beer off the door shelf. "Thanks, don't mind if I do, and I love you too." She sauntered over to the top wooden drawer, knowing she had to nudge it side to side a bit before yanking it out. She reached in, held the bottle with one hand, and popped its lid, which fell into her other hand below. She made an easy toss into the garbage can and then turned around to push the drawer back in using her back, continuing to lean on the counter.

"Don't go telling your Pop that Gram's buying you beer now," Pa mused.

Joan laughed. She decided the bag didn't need the added stress of turning it inside out. She had dropped a dot of dish liquid soap into the plastic bag and was swishing the suds around. After rinsing it, she reached up high and placed it on its side over one of the many horizontal wooden chopsticks that stuck out from their round base, which Pa had made. She turned to Gram and nodded at it. "Still going." They both smiled.

"So, Lady Joan, Lady Doris. How do you find the simple people of our land doing this fine day?" Gram asked, affecting a horrible fake English accent with her teacup raised and pinky extended.

HOLLYWOOD

Joe had told Joan that the river made national news and that downriver near the camps, it was getting crowded. "Nice enough people, no problems," he assessed. She'd be seeing more officers showing up and more protesters, "and more headaches all around," he added.

This morning, she left with her journal safely tucked in Pony, nestled against the precious cargo space under the seat. It had been demoted somewhat in importance by the treats Gram had set out for her in the famous Ziplock bag which was still in use and seemed to be on its way to setting a new world record in Joan's opinion.

Gram had wrapped two pieces of crunch cake for Joan. It was her favorite, and Gram's recipe added that special touch. A pound cake with a vanilla wafer crust, but there was something more to it. Maybe it was the amount of vanilla or the pecans in the crunch. Whatever it was, it tasted even better than when her mom made it from the same recipe passed down by Gram. By now Gram had learned it was best to pack two of whatever she wanted Joan to have for lunch or a snack on the road—one for Joan and one for her soon-to-be friend.

Gram was proud of the confidence and growth Joan had shown in the past couple of months. Pa had been right; that Pony was just what she needed. She thought about how little girls dream of having a pony, but she was pretty sure it wasn't quite like this one.

Pa strolled into the kitchen, walked right up to Gram, and planted a kiss on top of her head. "Mornin', Sunshine." He plopped down in his kitchen chair and found himself staring at a piece of crunch cake that Gram had carved into a heart shape. "What's this?" he asked. Gram sat beside him, reached her hand out, placed it atop his, gave it a pat, and then reached for the teapot in front of them to pour Pa a cup.

"You were right. That damned Pony has been great for her. The two of you are magical together, and I need to remember that your ideas create good things, really good things."

"Even a blind squirrel gets a nut once in a while," Pa replied warmly.

"How many times have I heard this? That squirrel must have a full belly by now!"

"Good ol' Mike Madden told me that. Have I ever told you that?" Gram shook her head as she rolled her eyes. Pa continued, "It'll be funny when we get really old, and you forget you ever heard it."

"What?" Gram asked with a mischievous grin.

"I said it'll—ohh, oh, real funny."

"Huh?" Gram pretended again like she was an old lady who couldn't hear.

"Wha—?"

Pony was parked by the "Pile Of Meow," as Joan had written about it in her journal, and she had recognized the sound of engines slowing down. She looked up to see two black vans pull over. It was the first time she felt nervous out here, perhaps because Joe had mentioned that things were heating up downriver. Here she was, miles from anyone in sight, and she felt a sudden urge to reach for her cell phone. She placed it just under the shelf of a nearby rock, within easy reach of a single tap that would call out to the sheriff, Doris, and initiate video and audio recording if something happened. She thought maybe she should have carried a knife or—oh, stop it. They don't know I don't have a gun, she reassured herself.

The vans had pulled over just past Pony and the Meow pile, but it seemed like the occupants hadn't noticed her. How could they not notice Pony? The driver of the first van, a woman, jumped out and unzipped her pants, crouching down in front of the van to relieve herself. It was a matter of urgency. When you gotta go, you gotta go. She pulled her pants back up and drove off with the second van following. Joan shook her head. "Weird," she said aloud. "Meow," a kitten nearby replied.

Joan didn't see Joe at the river's edge, but they did spot the two vans parked together. A large movie camera on a tripod had been set up in the gravel on a rubber mat. These people didn't seem scary in the sense of wanting to harm her. Instead, they appeared to be journalists—scary in a different way, as Pa would say. Joan unstrapped her small backpack from Pony's back and looked around. She spotted the Webcam, its small blue light blinking, indicating that it was on and recording. If anything were to happen, it would be captured. Pa, Gram, Mom, and Doris all knew where she went each day and Doris could even access the Webcam online. It was installed last month after a confrontation between one of the ranchers and a guard. Joan had met Miles that day; he was a handyman who could do just about anything. People hired him to get things done, like figuring out a way to install Webcams along the river and getting the necessary equipment. Pa could have done it, Joan thought. So, she had asked Miles if he knew Pa, and sure enough, Miles had learned welding from Pa, he said. Joan couldn't help but notice that the people with the vans either hadn't seen her yet or, if they had, hadn't acknowledged her presence.

She opened her thermos and took a sip, finding that Gram had made some lemonade. It was a pleasant surprise. Gram had replaced the water in the thermos, which Joan had filled earlier, with her homemade lemonade. It made sense considering the vanilla-flavored crunch cake combo, Joan thought. She put her cell phone in her pocket and left her backpack next to the rock she had been perched on. Walking over to the group of visitors, she knew not to startle them. The sound of her footsteps on the gravel would announce her approach. She stepped into the gravel a bit closer to the river and walked toward the small group who now looked up at her in shock.

"Hi there!" Joan waved, and one of the men nodded his mouth agape.

"I hope I didn't startle you," Joan said.

"Where'd you come from, the water?" one of the men asked.

"Ha, ha! Nope, I didn't think you all heard or saw me, did you? I rode up—" Joan pointed to Pony. "Yep, on a motorcycle."

"We didn't hear anybody. Whoa, you alone?" one of the women asked.

Joan decided not to answer that just yet. "You folks pulled over on the highway right in front of us a little while ago," she looked around for a response. "Well, it was a short stop," she added with a smile. "I live nearby. You all are media?"

The woman, who looked like the youngest of the five, replied, "We're here on location for STOP." Joan knew STOP, a non-profit organization called **S**top the **T**oxic **O**il **P**ipeline.

"I know what that is. You all know that downriver is where all the hubbub is?" Joan asked with a smile.

"We're here on purpose," she replied curtly.

"Oh, okay, cool," Joan responded. She turned and slowly walked back to her rock, opened her thermos and took a long sip. The coolness was lovely, especially on this warm morning. She leaned back admiring the alder leaves shaking in the morning breeze and thought about how Doris's dad might translate that into metalwork. Just as she was lost in her thoughts, she heard a car approaching. Looking up she saw another identical van coming down the steep approach to the riverbank lot. "Weird," she thought as she watched the van pull alongside the other two, blocking anyone's ability to turn around if they needed to. This kind of behavior was a bit irritating to the locals, but she also couldn't help thinking it felt very New York City, although that was no excuse. She smiled, realizing she had picked up some local habits, like using the word "hubbub" and such. As she was enjoying her own thoughts the passenger door of the van opened and a young man stepped out. He didn't look much older than she was, but he was tall with dark, well-coiffed hair that had clearly seen some styling that morning. He walked around the van pushing his sunglasses up onto his head as he looked directly at Joan. She thought to herself, "I guess I'm not invisible after all," and waved a polite "Hi" to him. He smiled and waved back walking over to her.

"Is that your Moto Guzzi?" he asked.

"Yep, that's my Pony," she nodded, smiling, fully aware of how it might sound to others.

"Is that a '72 Traveler?" he inquired further.

"Yep. With a modified carb and we installed an aftermarket electric start," she explained.

"That's a beauty. I have a '77 and a '79. There aren't many '72's still around."

"Nope. The '72s were known for breaking down. I read it's because of its failure in relational thoughtfulness in the motor design," sharing her knowledge and her interest was fun.

"Wow. Yeah," he nodded in agreement, clearly impressed. He couldn't hide his admiration for her. "Are you one of the protest campers or do you live out here?"

"Hmm, I guess I do live out here, for now, anyway. It's a long story. I just learned how to ride this summer from my grandpa. This was his bike back in '72," she explained. "I live in New York, but my family has deep roots here."

She nodded to the river noticing it seemed to have a smooth, rolling surface today. She turned away from the river, "And you? Your hair tells me you're not local," she teased with a playful smile.

He chuckled, looking at his own reflection in the water. "Yeah, I guess you could say I'm not from around here."

"Well," she continued, "if you were, we'd all know about you because then your hair would be the talk of the town."

He had what Joan would call 'beautiful looks.' His skin was smooth, and his eyes were a sparkly blue that seemed to capture the sun's rays and shine back with meaning. She had never seen blue eyes quite like his before. She figured he was someone famous visiting to support the river protesters and she liked him for that.

"Oh, this is great. You don't recognize me, do you? Or do you, and you're just being cool?" he asked.

"I say 'cool'," Joan laughed. "Not many of us say 'cool' around here," she added, playfully shaking her head.

"Hippie parents?" the young man asked, glancing up to see what had caught Joan's attention.

"Yep," she replied with a grin.

They shared a laugh.

"I'm Joan. Hi," she introduced herself.

"This is great. You're like my age and don't know me. I love it," he said, shaking his head, feeling more at ease by the moment.

"We can keep it that way, just don't tell me," Joan said playfully.

He laughed. "I'm Tony? Tony Misner?" He waited for the recognizable response.

Joan saw what he was doing. "So, YOU'RE Tony Misner?!" She laughed and then shrugged her shoulders and raised an eyebrow, curious.

"Oh no, I'm sorry. I haven't been able to introduce myself like a regular person like this for a long time now. It's—do you watch television, Joan?"

"Nope," she replied.

"Ha! That's so great. I don't either. I work in television. I'm in a series that's been on the air for a couple of years now.

It's crazy popular. I'm kind of a big thing right now. It won't last forever, just right now it is crazy. I just wrapped a film that has some buzz and that's fun."

"Ohhhhhh," Joan sang out her realization, pointing at him in fake recognition that he was "*THAT* Tony!" She clasped her hands together in mock excitement. And held her hands together with glee, pretending to be a fangirl. She teased, tilting her head and batting her eyes. Tony leaned back slightly, not quite sure how to react. Then Joan waved her hand," I'm just kidding. Not a clue as to who you are or your TV show. No offense," she added with a friendly smile.

They laughed.

Joan explained that she was raised without cable television; her parents considered it rubbish, so the family rented movies instead. She had seen some TV at friends' houses but generally agreed with her parents about its quality. She mentioned that she hadn't recognized him and hadn't seen him on YouTube either as her algorithm was mostly focused on old movies and motorcycle repair. She wondered if she was talking too much and decided to steer the conversation toward a practical matter, but couldn't think of one, so she just stopped weirdly which resulted in an uncomfortable silence.

Tony explained that he liked the fact she didn't recognize him as it allowed him to have a regular conversation. He was visibly enjoying the encounter and the break from his usual routine.

"Well, look at this," Joan said, spreading her arms to indicate the picturesque surroundings. "This is better than television, right?"

Tony enthusiastically agreed, "So refreshing." His perfect teeth made Joan conscious of her own, wondering if her teeth appeared less appealing in comparison.

Feeling like a host, Joan continued, "You're here to hide from your screaming fans, right?"

"Yesssss," Tony replied with a sigh of relief. He proceeded to remove his boots and socks, rolling up his jeans before walking to the river's edge. "Ahhh," he sighed contentedly, taking a deep breath. He glanced at Joan and gestured, inviting her to join him. Without hesitation, she followed. He noticed her prosthetic leg and she noticed him noticing, but neither of them made a big deal out of it.

"They're waiting for the right light, then I'm going to stand over there and make a fundraising speech about how fragile this ecosystem is and the threat of the oil pipeline. I'll most likely be working into the afternoon and then have to get back to L.A.," Tony explained.

"That's awesome that you're doing this," Joan replied, appreciating his commitment to the cause.

"Yeah, and it will help. I love that it will. I'm a product now, so when I have time, I use my product to be of service. I wish I had my bike here; we could go for a ride; you could show me around." Tony turned, opening his arms wide to encompass the beautiful surroundings. "It's so beautiful out here, even the drive up."

"I won't let anyone ride Pony, but yeah, in the future, if you come back, I can show you around. First, you'd want to meet Pa; he's sort of the 'OB1' around here," she emphasized, "He taught me everything I know about Moto Guzzis. We rebuilt it together. So much fun."

Tony chuckled, recognizing the Star Wars reference. "Yes, I see what you did there, Star Wars. I just have to say, it's nice to meet you, Joan. You're my Unicorn. I feel normal around you."

"That's good, normal. It's nice to meet you too, Tony. You know I'll be asking my friend Doris. who you are or maybe Google you. Is that okay with you?" He shrugged in response.

"She's going to be famous. She'll be diving in the next summer Olympics," Joan added proudly.

"Hey, no kidding. Wow. Really?" Joan nodded, confirming it. "Her name is Doris?" Joan nodded again.

They both watched the river in silence for a moment. Joan then remarked, "I guess we are both similar, we are set apart from most people. I like that. It must be really weird to be famous. Do you travel around a lot?"

"I doooo," Tony's voice trailed off sounding somewhat exhausted. "The hardest part is when I am followed by someone. It's a creepy feeling. Wigs and baseball caps work well.

"Whoa," Joan said, her eyes wide.

"Yeah, really. I have to or I wouldn't make it anywhere on time and it's hard to get around sometimes. I have Nick, my best friend; I hire him to play decoy for me when it's too much. Like another duck, he'll lead the press or fans away, looking like me, and then I sneak out." Joan's mouth was agape, listening in shock. "I just tell myself that it's a game, part of managing the product. Then I don't go all nuts. I've learned that it can be either a hassle or fun. Perspective, context, you know?" Joan nodded, looking down at the shallow water at her toes and how her toes, when slightly tapped against the sandy river floor, caused ripples on the water's surface.

"It's like riding a motorcycle," she noted.

"Exactly," Tony agreed. "Geez, I'm just yakking away here. You're so refreshing!"

"Yeah?" Joan asked.

"Yeah!"

"Weird. You have Nick, I have Doris. She and I are different from most of the girls here. We'd rather be outside than inside at a dance, or whatever." The conversation lapsed into silence again. "I don't know why I said that. I guess I am so thankful for my friendship with

Doris that I'm happy for you having Nick and for finding someone," Doris' thumbs pointed back at herself, "who doesn't recognize you or know who you are before you meet. Newsflash, in the rest of the world this would be normal. People meet each other, then they are recognizable."

Tony laughed, "Yeah, okay, that's good, yeah. I DO know about that." He laughed again, seemingly lost in thought, maybe reminiscing about his time in New Zealand or Australia when he could be normal without wigs and baseball caps.

Joan smiled and reached into her pack then gingerly unwrapped a bandana-wrapped treat. "Wow, what is that?!" Tony's eyes lit up.

"THIS, Mr. Hollywood, is one of my Gram's Oscar-winning performances. Gram's crunch cake!" Joan proclaimed proudly. "And this piece is from Gram to you. Enjoy!"

"Oh!" Tony stepped quickly forward, held out his hand and gave a slight bow in thanks. "Oh man, oh man, oh man, man, this is good!" Tony was enthused after taking a bite.

Just then a guy in long pants and a long-sleeved cotton t-shirt, clearly overdressed for the weather, jogged over. It was evident to Joan that he was part of Tony's crew. He was carrying three bottles of water and clearly looked hot. He stopped in front of them, pushed up his eyeglasses with the back of his wrist, since his hands were full, and handed the bottles of water to Tony.

"Thanks," Tony said, then turned to Joan. "Want water, Joan?" She shook her head and pointed to her thermos. He took one bottle. "Thanks," he said to the guy again before the crew member returned to his duties.

"Is that normal?" Joan inquired.

"It's kind of nice, sometimes," Tony replied.

"I think I'd like that, especially when I wanted cookies," Joan teased. "Are you wearing a microphone? How did he—?"

"They're keeping an eye on me. It's his job to do stuff like this, so I thank him. I'd rather be alone here with you, but we're on a job, at least according to the insurance company."

"Insurance company? Oh, right, the product is insured. I get it, I think," Joan said, understanding.

"Yeah, like that. The problem is, I'm not listened to very well. Like, I don't like to use plastic," Tony explained. He placed the plastic bottle at his feet. "On set, I have a trailer that's plumbed, and I have a water filter that I love. It's reverse osmosis. I miss it whenever I'm on the road. I'll carry this around today so that they don't keep bringing me plastic bottles. I want to create a paper disposable product. Why these things, right?" He seemed embarrassed.

"Right," Joan agreed. She handed him her thermos. "Here, Gram's lemonade. It goes great with the cake. I'm not sick, are you?"

"Nope, thanks," Tony said, taking a swig. "That's delicious."

"Yep," Joan replied.

She could hear Tony's phone buzzing, but she liked the fact that he chose to ignore it. It had been over an hour now and she noticed he was cute. Really cute. His hair barely moved, except when there was a breeze coming from behind him, which was a distracting phenomenon.

Joan was relieved when Tony relaxed enough to sit beside her and share the view. He smelled good, like fresh air but not outdoor fresh, she noted.

Two squirrels had been playing in front of the small group, running back and forth between two trees. Tony had been watching them as well. None of the crew looked up from their phones. Joan and Tony laughed and looked at each other realizing the absurdity of the situation.

"Your phone has been going off like crazy and you haven't pulled it out yet. Not addicted?" Joan asked.

"Addiction? Well yeah, it is a zombie-making drug, huh?" Tony nodded over to the group. They laughed. Tony reached into his light safari-style jacket pocket for a moment and turned it off. "Have you ever noticed not how many people walk around with their heads in their phones and then notice those that don't? Man," he said, shaking his head. Joan noticed that he looked affected by his own words, his head lowered, appearing somewhat sad. She looked down at their feet, watching Tony pick up and drop rocks with the toes of his right foot and then his left, back and forth.

"On a quiet set, there is always a phone suddenly going off it seems. It can really be a hassle. They make these cell blockers for areas in the studio to block out reception, but they don't stop personal alarms and other stuff. We have a production manager who walks around with a basket collecting phones as people arrive on set, and still, someone's phone will go off."

"What if there's an emergency?" Joan asked, concerned.

"There is a studio number everyone is supposed to give out for that. My family knows how to get a hold of me there; it's no big deal. But all this," Tony pointed to his phone in his pocket, "can wait until I get back on the plane tonight. Otherwise, on the road, Mom has all the numbers and knows how to track me down wherever I go. My mom's my manager."

Joan nodded. "Yeah, so's mine." They laughed. "I've had her for 15 years," they laughed again, "She's a keeper."

"Tony having just taken a bite, he motioned, pointing his thumb at himself and muffled through the crunch cake, '17.' He gulped, shook his head, and asked Joan, 'Does she get 15%?'"

"Huh?" Joan looked at Tony and realized he was serious. "Well, that's just sad."

"Remember, I'm also a product."

"Oh right, right... but that's just weird."

"Yeah, it's sooo weird," he said. "When the attention was pouring on me I felt I was drowning but just able to bob up and down for air until I was rescued by a cast member who sort of coached me through with tools. We sort of rebuilt my way of seeing the world. When I figured out that what others see is the product and not me unless I let them in to see me. I could surf the attention, you know? Instead of feeling drowned by it."

"What happens when you want to do something else?"

"Man, Joan, for someone who doesn't know the business, you understand it a lot. That's just it. If I decided to quit and do something else, there would be a bunch of people that I would be putting out of work. I'm a business, and I have some responsibilities I don't want."

"Oh, Pa says I have no problem going deep as a well as fast as a hummingbird. Sorry if I'm prying. It's kinda my thing now. People. People are awesome," Joan smiled.

"People," Tony sighed and shook his head, "I don't know if they are real with me or want my product, you know?"

"How long have you been-uhm- 'famous'?" Joan asked using air quotes and leaned back against the rock behind her back, again looking up at the sun peeking directly through the alders. Tony followed, tapping his sunglasses down to cover his eyes. Joan took a sip from her thermos. "Hmm?" The thermos top squeaked, and Joan stopped turning it. She placed it between them, then opened her pack and pulled out two snap-lid containers. She turned them both over to see the contents through the glass.

"I started doing commercials when I was 4. I'll be 17 this November."

"November what?" Joan asked.

"The 6th."

"I'm the 8th!" Joan smiled.

"Oooo, Scorpios, no wonder we can talk so real, huh?"

"Yeah, cool!"

"Yeah, so, uhm, I started in commercials when I was 4 and then some small roles in films. I've always been working.

I mean around school hours... well, they have school on set too."

"So, let me get this straight. I'm picturing Hollywood sets I see in the movies, right?"

Tony nodded. "Yeah, pretty much. It's kinda more like a giant construction site.

"And then there's a school?"

"Well, so, okay." He grabbed a stick close by and drew in the gravel a big square with small squares. "So there's like a set, see? Actors' trailers are here, sometimes here. This might be a stage here and here if more than a couple scenes are being shot. Or there's a stage here being constructed for us, so we are here for now, then there." His stick was pointing from box to box. "Over here next to the trailers might be a trailer ya know a container on a trailer bed that gets moved around to whatever lot needs it. Kids go to get, like, homeschooled. It's super insulated, really quiet, like a tiny library. It's nice. Studios are loud. Cranes, forklifts, heavy things rolling. It's like a construction site, and then, to get away from it all, you can pop in here if it's not being used and hide out. If you worked there, I wouldn't tell you that. My little secret and all."

He was delightfully animated now and seemed comfortable. He looked like he'd been coming here as long as she had, Joan thought. Look at him, pants rolled up, drawing with a stick. "If it wasn't for his hair," Joan added, but she liked his hair. She could see over it now; it had swoops going one way and another. Whoops, she realized she wasn't listening. "I have two more years before I'll have my B.A. It's mostly online, but real transferable credit. I get tests proxy and my papers read in there. There's a professor who works at all levels of education. He's hired by the Studio. I think it's a great job, maybe something I'd do if I wasn't acting. Mom says I'd be bored. I don't know. I like stuff like this too. Conservation; waking up the zombies to what's happening."

"A life of service, eh?" Joan asked.

"Yeah, that's nice, 'A life of service,'" Tony said as he looked up to the treetops above. "What do you want to do, Joan?"

"Your life seems so full already!" She noticed she hadn't removed her boots yet today. She was comfortable all this time without having to work on it. "Interesting," she made a mental note to journal about this. Tony was sketching lines in the gravel.

"I need to think about that. I guess it's time I do that," she answered him.

"You're my age? Wait, no, you said 15. The kids I work with started about 8th grade, so I guess yeah, you should if you want to. It seems so personal."

"*My* manager thinks I should follow in her footsteps and go medical."

"Manager!" Tony laughed. "You crack me up, Joan."

"You too."

"Have you noticed they are still on their phones?" Tony nodded over towards them. "They're like in their 20s and 30s. I just don't want to be all sucked into my phone when I'm their age."

"That's just it, it's like what is it I don't want?" Joan felt she figured something out here and pushed on. "Maybe if I list all the things that bother me, I'll figure it out."

"So, I can tell you what Tyz taught me. Take money out of it, pretend it is a moneyless world," Tony advised.

"I get that, okay," she started to ask herself just that, and Tony held up his hand.

"K, there's more, it's three parts. This is so cool I get to share this, okay - okay so it's a moneyless world. And now you figure you have a 100-year life. So, you take your 15 from that and have 85 left, right?" Joan nodded. "Sounds like a lot, right? 85 years in weeks is..let's keep it simple, is, say 4400 weeks left to your life. Just being real. Check this out now, that 4400 weeks isn't what's up because we spend about 12 hours of our day in self-care, such as sleeping, eating, personal care, and maybe more. So now get this, 2200 weeks left for you to live actively available. 2200 weeks."

"Oh, my Gawwwwd, I never turned math on myself before. 2200 is not a lot of time."

"It's 184,800 hours -about 21 years"

"Whoa"

"Yeah. And that's to age 85."

"Whoa"

"Yep. Shocking. Rough numbers but close enough. So, then you ask yourself, one, what is it I care about most, two, how many years do I have to help that cause, and three, what is the best way I can be of service in my 85 remaining years?"

"I love that! I must write that down.

"I'll text it to you tonight if you want. And also, how many weeks left in those 85 years left. I can scare myself into motivation if I don't stop, ha-ha. Oh, warning though, if you do the week's math, it is freaky because we can all brush away years, years are long, right? But when I did the weeks, it really woke me up. And it's not really to 85 active years of life, there are maybe sick weeks and perhaps you retire from whatever early."

"Thanks, Tony," Joan said thoughtfully, lost in his questions. The van crew began to scurry like mice now, so something was up. Joan watched big discs appear from a couple of large, folded fan-like things, and then one of the people attached a cord to the camera from something box-like in their hand, holding it out. He waved. "We're good now," Joan could hear him say over the alder leaves, as Tony played with the stick in the gravel.

"Looks like they're doing it over there. You have to go?"

"Soon, it won't take long, though. It's crazy. Most of my world is waiting around like this. But this is the best set ever, thanks to you Joan."

Joan noticed he kinda sparkled when he looked at her then, and her body reacted in a high-pitched tinge. She liked him a lot. But was that the product sparkling or Tony? She decided to "cool her jets," as Joan's mom told her once before. Tony was leaving tonight.

"Oh, here. Let's do this now, okay?" He reached back into his jacket pocket, pulled out his phone and turned it on. Handing it to Joan, "I'll text you right now. You'll see a San Francisco area code; that's me. Oh, and I have a fake public name. Bob. That's Bob with one O. Please don't tell anyone." Joan shook her head in agreement.

Joan laughed, and so did Tony. "My full name is Bob Withoneo."

They burst into laughter together and one of the women walked over. "We're ready for makeup and they're good to go, okay?" Joan was surprised at the amount of respect the woman was giving Tony using her professional tone of voice.

"Thanks," he nodded, and off she walked back to the group. "I gotta go over there, but I'll be here if you know what I mean."

Joan didn't really, but nodded yes, smiling as he walked away. He turned to catch her smiling after him and smiled. He stopped next to one of the group and pointed at the van that blocked the lot. The next thing Joan saw was someone hopping in the van and moving it into the lot. She was thankful for Tony catching on to the obvious which others had failed to see.

Joan watched for a while. Tony seemed natural; he stood there next to the river's edge with his jeans rolled up, and he said something to a camera. In no time he was back at the rock.

"See?" Tony shrugged, "It's like '80 percent waiting and 20 percent doing.'"

"That's it, eh? Wow, is it like that on your TV show?"

"Pretty much for the first half of the day, yeah, then it's more like a play... mm, sort of. You can come watch anytime. Just let me know. If you want, I mean."

"That's so weird, Tony."

"Yep," he said.

PIE

Joan was writing the three questions Tony taught her in her journal. She had watched the efficient van gang of zombies pack up quickly and hit the road. Tony and Joan gave each other a quick hug and waved goodbye, one that Joan could still feel as she was writing in her journal.

"Bob Withoneo," Joan said aloud to herself inside her helmet just for a laugh. "Wow." She said aloud. And then again, a moment later. Pony sounded great on the ride home; the air seemed to sparkle in the sun rays that had made their way through the poplar canopy. Joan slowed down, needing extra time to settle down before reporting this to Doris when she came over after practice. She decided not to arrive home until after she had figured that out. Tony was some big star and Doris probably knew who he was. If he has screaming fans, the last thing Joan wanted was to have strangers asking her about him if the word got out and she didn't want Doris distracted from her own goals.

Joan pulled over in a sun-drenched patch of warmth to give Gram a call. She felt it getting cooler and the sun was about to pass over the ridge. She had been there longer than usual. She thought Gram might be wondering where she was, so she set Pony's kickstand, got off, lifted the seat and grabbed her cell phone. Waiting for her were 4 messages, all from Doris. The first one had arrived 55 minutes earlier.

1- "Hey, call home. Gram's worried you're with the protestors. Fight there today and rumors of a shooting."

2- "YOU HOO."

3- "I'm thinking your phone is off. I called. Ugh."

4- "Pa and I are heading out to look for you. 'Concerned,' he says. TEXT ME."

"Oh m'gawwd," Joan said aloud. She texted Doris: "I'm calling Gram. All's well. I'm not downriver. I'll call you next."

"Gram, you okay? I'm sorry, my phone was on Pony. I was too far away to hear it ring."

"Oh, Joan! Are you near the Protest? There was worry and tension in Gram's voice that bothered Joan. She began packing Pony just then."

"No, Gram, I'm at the Kayak put-in upriver. What happened? Doris texted there was a shooting?"

"Blaise said the town is buzzing about some young man getting shot, an accident maybe, he isn't sure. Just in case, we wanted you nowhere near there. Are you coming home soon?"

"Yes, Gram, I'll come right home. I didn't hear a shot, not even a Sheriff siren. Must be farther off. I'm sorry I scared you. I'll keep my phone closer from now on. I'll call Doris; she says she's with Pa, and they can relax too. Geesh."

"Geesh, alright... supposed to be a peaceful protest. Peaceful," Gram's voice sounded disappointed and quieter now.

"Okay, love you, bye," and Joan hung up.

"We're heading back home now," was how Doris answered her phone. She could hear they were in the truck driving somewhere.

"So, rumor or someone actually got shot?" Joan asked.

"After pie," Joan heard Pa groan loudly in the background. Joan knew they were driving in the truck by the sound of the passenger door rattling in the background.

"After pie Pa says we're heading home" Doris reported, "That means the bakery maybe?" She looked at Pa who nodded. "Yep, the bakery Joan. Maybe Jenny or Catherine knows the scoop. I'll ask around. Nothing on Insta."

Joan and Pony headed out. Nothing unusual happened on the road back and Joan noticed that her head was being interrupted with flashes of memories of her time with Tony earlier. Flash, his hair. Joan would smile and then remember to focus on the ride, and nothing else. Flash - his looking at her that way that made her tingle then, and now. Re-focus.

When she rode Pony into her stall, Doris was already reading a book in Pa's shed chair. It was all wobbly, and if you leaned back on it and it rolled there was a very good chance you were going to end up in some sort of disaster.

"Hey," Doris waved.

Joan pulled off her helmet, "Hey!" and gave her head a good scratch and her hair a few passes of finger-combing. "Did you ask around?"

"Shelley said that Savanna was there taking photos when it happened. It's no one we know. Some kid from Colorado, camping at the river, accidentally shot himself, grazing his stomach, but he'll be fine. There was a fight but it wasn't physical, just words as usual. I heard that some protesters get up in their faces and instead of singing or quietly talking, they get carried away and mouth off to one another."

"Well, that doesn't sound peaceful AT ALLLL!" Joan emphasized. "This whole thing is crazy. Are they going to block the construction through winter? This is like Standing Rock all over again." Joan hung her helmet over Pony's throttle using the helmet's face cradle, and she and Doris were now walking across the yard to Gram's kitchen. They opened the door and let it slap behind them just about the same moment Joan said, "Pie."

"You want some, Joan?"

"I've never seen you eat someone else's pie, Gram!"

"Me neither," Doris added, opening the fridge and lifting a root beer off the door shelf.

Gram and Pa didn't say anything, just took another bite while smiling at one another.

"Strawberry Rhubarb," Gram mumbled, smiling and finishing chewing. "It's my comfort food. When your dad was born your Pa brought me a slice of pie; cherry. Your father was a big baby, and I was in a lot of hurt down there afterward. For some reason, I took a bite of that pie and felt a bit better. Since then when there is trouble, Pie." Pa was stirring honey into his cup real slow and looking at Gram with love in his eyes.

"Eww, get a room," Doris said. Joan laughed.

"Pie! Okay then, Pie!" Joan took two small dishes down from the open cupboard behind her. Ignoring Gram and Pa's love gazing, Joan rolled her eyes to Doris.

"Hey, have you heard of Tony Misner?"

Doris' eyes bulged. "The movie star? Well duh, who hasn't ? "

Joan quickly changed the subject. "How'd practice go?"

"Nailed it twice. I'm close. Coach started me on a back 2 1/2 pike, yeah, I already got too close and broke two toes. "Doris lifted her right foot up, wincing a little and everyone winced right along with her. The two toes adjacent to her big toe were wrapped together in gauze except for the tops of the toes. Even with her tan skin, the toes looked bruised and purple. The bandages already looked old. She had obviously been diving with it and it was dirty from the day.

"Ouch cha chaaa, Dodo!" Joan winced. "Ughk, I don't know how you can do that and keep diving."

"Happens to everyone. Coach just has us get right back up on the board. If you dive through the pain a couple of times right away it doesn't hurt so bad later," Doris let out a big root beer burp.

"DORIS!" Gram reacted with a short shout.

"Sorry, Gram," Doris responded quickly

"Seriously now," Joan sided with Gram. "I think Dodo spends too much time alone over there, eh Gram?" Joan asked with a laugh

"Well, some manners could keep her company. My word, Dodo!"

"Sorry, Gram."

Joan just laughed again. She looked at Pa, who was still making eyes at Gram. She looked at Doris, who was picking out the rhubarb and eating it on its own now. "Mom and I don't waste moments anymore. I need to say something before this moment slips by. It's something we started back when we lost Dad." The room was silent. Pa stopped stirring his cup and leaned back, shifting his gaze to Joan.

Joan had the room's attention. "It's just, well, I love you all. I can't think of anything better than this right here and now. Thanks for being so nice to me, and I love you all." Joan teared up, and Doris stood up and gave her a squeeze.

"Ah, yay!" Gram toasted with her teacup.

"This is some strong pie!" Pa said, throwing a wink at Joan and they both smiled.

Joan had been on the phone explaining her crazy day to her mom who was in a private call room this time. Her hair was down and she looked tan and relaxed, which helped Joan relax.

"Then Gram said Pa brought her pie when Dad was born," Joan continued, sharing her day's events.

"He brought pies to Dad's celebration of life at our house in the city. Do you remember that?"

"Pie. Umm, I don't remember foods, but I do remember the sadness on everyone's faces. I had already done my crying by then. I was in my wheelchair, and my leg extending out in its brace made corners hard for people to navigate around I remember. I positioned my chair near the front entrance against the wall to be clear. I remember thinking the air seemed heavy like the sadness on faces," Joan and her mom looked into each other's eyes in silence for a moment, then Joan smiled, took a refreshing breath and continued.

"I had one of our 'don't waste a moment' moments tonight in the kitchen. I wish you were there. Everything just felt so, like, thankful to me that I stood up and announced that I loved everyone," Joan blushed as she shared this with her mom, as if it were an accomplishment.

"That's amazing, Jo-Jo," her mom smiled into the computer. "So how are you doing, any episodes?"

"Nope, kind of even forget sometimes."

"And this Bob kid?"

"I'll tell you more about him when I see you at Christmas if you still get to come home?"

"We think so. So far so good."

"He's cute Mom, super cute actually."

"Joan?"

"He already flew home to Los Angeles."

"Ouch. Sorry."

"Oh, it's even silly to think about. And with only 100 years left, I'm running out of time to think about stuff. Gotta be choosy you know."

Joan's mom smiled. "How's Doris?"

"She has Olympic coaching staff coming and going a lot now. She said that Coach says they want her, and that means full scholarship offers will be coming soon!"

"We have to do something special to celebrate when I come out, okay? We need to think about this. Use the card I gave you; I added more money to it and you haven't spent all of the last months so treat yourself and Doris more. You two have been so serious, I don't want you to rush your teenage years. Have some fun!'"

Joan's phone buzzed, and she looked over at it: "Hi, it's me, Bob. Want to play Words with Friends?" Joan raised her eyes back up to her mom's.

"Hey Mom, have you heard of homeschooling online? Tony said he's been doing that since he was a kid and now, he's in college early. He checks in with a professor who watches him take tests for classes and stuff. I Googled and found this website that has a list of accredited online schools. What I read is that if I am self-motivated and self-disciplined which I am, I can jump ahead further than if I go to a regular school."

"Okay that sounds exciting, I can see you are. Would you miss school activities?"

"I dunno. I don't think so, but I hadn't thought about that. I will though. I'd rather focus on the work and be social later if that makes sense. I guess maybe that's backward? I feel like I'm in a steady flow. Gram says to be careful not to push the river, so I'll sleep on this some more, Mom. Joan realized that maybe for Tony, meeting her was like he said; really refreshing. He wasn't around many people his age who didn't know him.

It was another 20 minutes before Joan signed off with her mom who promised to Skype again the next Saturday. She was in a remote area now and they used Satellite but understood it as a limited resource. The military asks families to keep conversations brief but medical personnel get extra time. They said constant contact was important the more stress the job entailed over there. Joan received newsletters from the MFF, a military forum on family in the military. They shared the latest medical research on PTSD. How to prevent it and prompts to assist in how to communicate better with loved ones abroad. Since Joan signed up for it, it became a game she and her mom played sometimes. Joan would try a suggestion from the forum during a Skype call, attempting to be smooth, but her mom had caught her every time so far. Joan figured she'd probably never be able to slip one of those lines past her mom.

"Hi Bob, :-)," Joan typed, smiling at his Bitmoji riding a plane and waving. "I was Skyping with my mom overseas when you texted. I'm free to play now."

"Cool!" Tony responded with a Bitmoji of himself riding a plane and waving. "Wheels down in 20."

She opened her Words with Friends app and texted him the scorpion emoji. "Ready."

NAILED IT

Scrunched into the blanket bundle she had cocooned herself in, Joan looked up at Doris's dad next to her. He looked like an alien with his striped puffy jacket and Elmer Fudd hat. It was an unexpectedly chilly September morning, and her ear was ringing thanks to the whistle he sent out without warning, cheering Doris on.

"Oh, I'm sorry about that Sweetie!" he said, reaching out with both arms to give her a quick hug before returning to his hands-in-pockets, legs outstretched position. One leg shaking, and a big smile on his face. They were all spread out on a patch of grass hill above the diving pool along with other families and fans.

They had piled into Pa's truck together – Doris' dad, Gram, Pa, Joan, and a fully charged cell phone with a battery pack as a backup. Joan was determined to catch this on video. This was Doris' time to shine. Joan couldn't tell where these two Olympic scouts were after scanning the bleachers and the people on the hill like Doris' dad and her. Nothing like a clipboard or notepad was noticeably attracting her attention. She looked above and behind them at the small line of cars along the fence line. Gram and Joan caught each other's eyes and Gram smiled and waved from Pa's truck. The two of them had wisely chosen to watch from there as did many others in cars and trucks along the fence line. Joan waved back, smiling and giving a thumbs up. They looked warm and comfortable. Joan was so proud of everyone for being here. She knew Doris had dives that would blow them away.

The divers didn't seem bothered by the cold; they were bouncing on the boards and diving just fine. They stayed in the water along the side of the pool until their last name was called. Joan learned that the water was kept at about 80 degrees, so they were probably just fine. Steam rose from the diving pool. When a diver would pop up out of the water their body would throw an aura of steam. Doris' dad and Joan agreed it looked super eerie like a sci-fi movie and they were enjoying that perspective as entertainment during the boring easy dives. Doris and her dad exchanged a short whistle now and then. The sun was out, but it was still chilly on the hillside. Joan noted a chilly breeze. "Gram says Global Warming brought the frost early this year," Joan reported to Doris' dad.

This was it, the 3-meter back 2 1/2 layout. And a flawless execution! Followed by her full-twisting 1 1/2 pike on the

1-meter board which received 9's and a 10. But it was the 3-meter reverse 1 1/2 pike that stole the show. All the judges awarded her perfect 10's, and the crowd erupted in a standing ovation! Cars parked on the street hill overlooking the pool honked in celebration. Her dad was whistling wildly, as Doris triumphantly punched the air and waved to everyone from the water. Her coach leaned down, and they exchanged high-fives. Both Joan and Doris' dad jumped up and down, cheering. Joan plopped down on the grass in awe, acknowledging that she was witnessing her best friend's rise to stardom.

MANIFESTATION

"This is it; you know?" Doris said, pacing her bedroom as she had been for countless laps, as Joan watched her, smiling for so long and so hard that her mouth muscles were hurt. Doris had just left the meeting with her parents, Coach, and TeamUSA's scout who were still saying their goodbyes in the living room.

"I'd heard about college scholarships for diving and figured yeah, maybe some money, but Coach said I'll be getting calls now offering a full free ride!? Four years of pretty much my pick! All I wanted to do was feel what it's like to fly and now look at this. Crazy."

"College?!" Joan exclaimed. "Really, college? Blah Blah college DoDo—Hellloooo?? You are going to be in the U.S.A. OhhhhhhhLYMPIC TEAM, Doris!"

"Hold on, hold on, don't make me pee my pants. He said I'm invited to the trials; there are kids from all over trying out. They can probably do quads-"

"Excuse me? No, nah uh uhh. This is about YOU, Doris Dobi. YOU were just - okay 'invited' - to be a-okay 'possible'- teammate on our U-S-of—Doh, we KNOW you are on the team. We are making sure of that." Joan jumped on Doris' bed, pretending it was a podium, and looking up at the flag they raised above in the award ceremonies. "OLYMPIC TEAM!"

They both screamed then hushed each other realizing the meeting in the other room might have heard them.

Joan's phone went off. It was Tony. Her phone still displayed, "Bob," and she always laughed inside when she saw, "Bob," and would think about Tony when she was around someone named "Bob." She read the text out loud to Doris.

" Hey there. Got your texts about Doris' 10's! Please tell Doris I think she's phenomenal and congrats!"

"Aw, he's so nice. Tell him thanks and I look forward to meeting him… somedayyy?" Doris comically raised her eyebrows in a flirtatious teasing way to Joan.

Joan shook her head and took a breath. "I mean really, DoDo, like, just, wow, so great!" She shook her head, smiled, and stood up, "One day at a time, okay? Colleges have guidance counselors and stuff like that. We don't have to do it all alone."

Doris sighed, "Right, okay, yeah, that's right. Geez. I'm used to figuring out stuff pretty much alone, y'know?"

Joan sat next to Doris, "Well, yeah, but real life is looking really different than college maneuvering and diving practice. You'll have coaches and personal coaches to answer questions, and we're welcome to ask all the questions we want, okay? I mean maybe whatever you do now will help me when I'm doing it next. I'm right after you in school, after all."

They sat in silent contemplation for a bit then Joan added, "I have no idea what I'm going to major in..." Joan was lost again, shaking her head, staring into space.

"Joan!"

"Yeah, thanks, okay yeah," she giggled.

"One day at a time," Doris said, throwing an arm around Joan's shoulder and playfully swiping her bangs across her face. "You're freaking out, Joan." One day at a time, one thought at a time." The pizza timer went off with a loud "buzz."

"And in this moment: Pizza." She took both of Joan's shoulders and shook them, "PIZZZZZZAAAAAHHHH!"

Later that night at 11 pm, Joan's time, their scheduled Friday night Skype call Joan shared her college concerns and thoughts about her major with her mom.

"You've always asked me about blood and operations. I can set up a tour or arrange for you to shadow a nurse or doctor at the hospital if you want to look and feel what my world is like. The important thing is to be happy at what you're doing. So don't think it's what I want for you or what others want for you. Take some alone time each day and make notes of your interests and what you like and - ."

"-and what I care about-." Joan interjected, nodding along.

"Right. Maybe spend some time each day until we chat again, and I'll check in with you. It's okay if you have a lot of notes or none at all. Don't put pressure on yourself. This is just the beginning. There is no race Honey. This is the start of thinking about the process of entering a chosen next process towards finding your focus. You are ahead. If you weren't, I'd be all up and down your spine, you know that. Just relax and get to know yourself, open up to yourself like you do with others when you are exploring with Pony, but within you now. Okay? No pressure."

"Thanks - Okay good, I can do that."

"All right! Don't push too hard. Remember in therapy how, when you'd push yourself too hard, you'd create a longer healing process?" Joan nodded, remembering how pissed off she was at herself for thinking doing extra exercises would help her leave the hospital faster, and instead, it meant more weeks due to strains or some sort of fiber rips here and there she had caused with overexertion.

"Ack! Okay. Yeah, Mom," just the mention of it brought those memories right back.

"You got this Sweety, just keep communicating. We both know no matter how hard it is to unlock, that the key is strength through softness. Right?"

"I love you, Mom," she nodded in agreement.

"Love you back smack!" She automatically answered, kissing her hand and throwing that kiss through the computer screen into Joan's smile.

Joan closed her laptop and laid back on her bed staring at the ceiling and thinking. "Strength through softness," she softly repeated.

She woke the next morning in that same position, still in her clothes, her laptop next to her. Time had just slipped by, paying no mind to anyone being ready for its movement, she thought. She changed her clothes, even though it made sense to just keep wearing what she had on. "It's efficient," she mused to herself. "Sleeping in clothing that isn't dirty yet seemed smart. It makes for getting ready faster," she continued while making her bed. "It makes me feel organized and starts my day off with an accomplishment," Mom had told her years ago while putting fresh sheets on her bed. Joan agreed and followed suit.

Joan padded quietly down the hall to brush her teeth in the tiny bathroom she had grown to adore, with its convenient shelves and drawers. She loved how Pa decided to make a vertical drawer where her toothpaste and toothbrush were stored. She rested her morning eyes on the little knob that had a small, blue lavender blossom smack dab in the middle. She had always brushed her teeth the same way each time as directed by her mother, for efficiency and success. Joan liked a lot of the soldier-themed approaches, like keeping a sense of humor when things go bad and looking for greater humor, the greater the bad becomes. It had really helped Joan in her recovery. She remembered Doctor Doug telling her that we still don't know the human body, not entirely.

"For instance," he said, "Scientists know that when we set a broken bone which requires bone growth between two ends, the first cell appears exactly in the middle, in the space that lies between the two ends which are needed to come together. And that's not all. They don't know why or how that first cell gets there."

THOUGHTS ARE THINGS

Pa was sitting at the small kitchen table. The sun's rays bathed him in light, as though it was sitting at the table with him. She poured herself a glass of juice and sat down across from Pa, opened her algebra book and placed it on the table as she sipped her juice. It had become a natural routine for her. Both were quiet, and the only sounds in the room were the humming of the refrigerator with Pa stirring his tea.

"So, listen," Pa broke the silence. "Your mom called me." Joan looked up at him and searched his face for any signs of concern or curiosity. "She says you'd like to stick around here longer and maybe until she comes home for good? She says you and Doris being in different schools means you won't be having her around with you. How you feelin' about that?"

"Huh. So You and Mom talk behind my back? I'm not feeling good about that, Pa."

"Silly, your mom and I have been talkin' behind your back since before you were even born. Get over it. That's just how the cookie crumbles."

"Oh. K. Well, what do you mean, then? I don't understand the question?" Joan took another sip of her juice but this time she drank it with more reverence.

"Eat much?" Pa asked with a chuckle.

"Real funny."

"Yer mom, Gram, and I think it would be fine for you to hang out here and do your schooling at home. Whatcha all call it..., 'online'?" Joan raised her eyebrows in surprise.

"Really?"

"Well, you're doing so good. You've got stronger, thicker, smarter and spunkier. You still have those little monkey hands but if you're here, then those kids won't tease you and all." Pa smiled. "The thing is, this is a grown-up decision we're asking you to make. Serious stuff. Your mom said it's a difficult demanding online program she'd put you in, but with your self-drive in combination with your New York credits, it might just be enough to raise you to Doris' level by next year."

"What?" Joan blinked in disbelief.

"Difficult. That's the word you didn't hear right? Or did you hear the word 'Difficult'?"

"All school is difficult, Pa."

"It's the way your mom said it that should scare you."

"Oh, I know what you mean. "Joan slumped into the chair back.

"The thing is, kiddo, it means all those kids will miss out on getting to know you. Granted, they don't know what they're missin' if they haven't met you in town, but I don't see you bringin' any of those kids around here. Am I right?"

"Yeah, Pa. Doris and I are partners in crime, homeys in the hood, salt and peppahhhhh." Joan took another sip. The silence was back, but now Joan felt a buzz, or maybe she could hear it in the room. "So does this mean I would take the classes here and hang with you and Gram?"

"And the Olympian."

"Heh heh, yeah, our Olympian. All the AP online courses for a year?"

"At least the first semester, to try out if you like it. Joan, you are an intelligent and wise young woman, and we don't want anything but the best for you. Your mom seems to think you have it in you to do this. If it were up to me, I would choose school with the other kids because I was always the kid who needed approval from others to keep on keepin' on. But listen, you are self-motivated and seek what's around the bend before it even comes at you," Pa tapped his spoon on the cup's edge., "That's already a strong, successful tool in life that not everyone has in them. School won't teach you that; you either have it or you don't."

"What does Gram think?"

"What does Gram think about what? It's so quiet out there; I can hear you through the windowpane." Gram appeared, her basket full of fresh produce and kicked off her Mudders. She spilled the contents onto the counter like a painter's cornucopia. An array of squashes, potatoes, onions, leeks, and Joan's favorite, shishito peppers.

"Good morning! Wow, Gram, what a harvest!"

"Would you like to help me make soup today?"

"Yes, please! I'll roast the shishitos for sure, mmhmm. Pa said you all have been talking about my schooling online here if I want."

"I was thinking about this in the garden. I know you can get credit for working in the community with work experience, it's similar to what Doris and you both did that art project for school credit. Like that, but out in the community. You could meet more people. Maybe a few hours at the newspaper, or a store you are interested in. Make money for college. It might be good. It's different, but really good, I think. I'm not a kid though and that means dances and football games, those things the school has as events you won't be attending unless invited by Doris, you know."

"Pa added, 'What you don't know can't hurt you.'"

"I love the idea of being on my own studying. My school in New York is a pod school and I had a hard time concentrating there. I haven't been looking forward to going back to school at all. I remember I really liked studying alone in the hospitals. I could think better there, I kind of had my own quiet office. I was getting A's, and that's when I was first put into AP courses."

"That's what your mom said," Gram said.

"This talking behind my back is creepy," Joan announced with a serious tone. "All this college talk going around. Dodo with her full scholarship too."

"What's creepy is the thought of a little monkey like you in the big college jungle soon enough."

"You might have a scholarship in your future. Who knows what opportunities you might create for yourself? We just have to do our best and forget the rest." Gram smiled at Pa, then added, "Mmhmm, and as my Grandpa Paul used to say to my Gramma Bev, 'You get damn little out of life, and most of it is what you eat, so let's get somethin' on the table, Bevvie.'"

"Huh?" said Joan.

Gram grabbed a leek and bonked Pa on the top of his head. "You sure you want to be around THIS longer, Joan? Please! Now what do you want, crazy man? How about some garlic eggs?"

Joan looked over at Pa, who winked at her, and replied to Gram, "Yes, ma'am, I'd be honored to be egged by you."

Joan didn't wonder at all about that. It was a no-brainer; she loved being around these two. She also enjoyed the long hours when she was left on her own. This was her favorite place to live so far. Back East, at home, she was reminded of how much she missed her dad. It seemed everything she looked at had a memory involving him. Even the hospital was the same hospital he was brought to. Out here, she had found an emotional break.

She and Pony would have another month, maybe two before it was too cold for their morning rides. Gram had knitted Joan the best neck warmer; wool with enough cotton in it to keep it from being itchy. For now, it was all she needed for extra warmth this fall.

She checked her email to find that while she slept her mom had sent her a letter suggesting what Pa had just told her. She felt a little bad for having thought her mom was not involving her. All this time the email with a lot more information had been there since 2:01 am. She began clicking on the links her mom had sent and reading about these courses, credits, and requirements. She looked into the parameters and choices regarding what was called the "Fast Track" program. There were community business plans where she could get credit and a part-time job.

"Whoa. Paid for getting credits!" she exclaimed in surprise. Other than that, she could be anywhere and still be in class. "Nomadic Studies" it was called. This felt very doable. If she was working under a certified or licensed manager of any field she chose, field credit could be given after she turned in an essay about the experience.

Joan stayed in and decided she'd smell the onions first before heading in to help Gram. She might even wait for Gram to call out for help because this was really important. She was deeply focused inside the website planning out her possible routes. Reminding herself again and again as she continued with the maximum credits for minimal effort. Finally, she wondered, "Could I graduate in 16 months!?" She shook her head in wonder. "Is that right?" she asked aloud. She ripped a blank page from her journal and wrote it all down, like a graph, organizing and repeating mentally what she wrote as she wrote it.

Paper in hand, she jumped into Gram's kitchen. Pa was outside along the old grapevine, probably looking at old growth or new growth; she couldn't figure out how they could both tell which to prune. She did know she loved the seedless green grapes they produced and remembered that every gardener's tip in one season wasn't ever accepted by everyone, ever.

Gram had told Joan, "The garden is a journey."

"Gram, I'm pretty sure I did these numbers right. If I worked hard for 16 months in that 'Fast Track' program, I'd graduate in 16 months. 16!"

"So that's where you've been," Gram said with a knowing smile. "Your Pa and I sat down and figured it would be 14 months, 5 semesters early. Did you include the community work program credits I mentioned? An easy miss."

"14 months, Gram, 5 semesters, 4 if they allow me into statistics, and then Doris and I would be at the same levels. Maybe we could go to college together as roommates. I think I can do it!"

"Are you allowing time in there for a cold or the flu? And what about some vacation time?" Gram asked.

"I hadn't thought of that! Even with that added in, say a month or two?" Joan contemplated.

Gram nodded, shrugging one shoulder. "That's only a semester difference or so."

"14 months can be a long time. Try to make it fun JoJo. Talk it over with Dodo JoJo, "Gram smiled and winked, "Dodo will think of things to consider that you and I may not think of.   You might make it through in less time depending on your individual placements in the classes. Read the fine print again. But Joan? Stay loose JoJo", Gram smiled having had a sing-songing of their nicknames and watching Joan's eyeball roll, "Please peel those squash; we'll roast them on the wood stove first."

"Yes, Chef."

"Thank you, Chef."

"Here's Gram's container. Dad and I loved it last night. Mom always says we aren't supposed to return an empty container, so I asked Dad for something, and he said to give you this." Doris nodded, implying Joan should open it.

Joan popped the Tupperware lid open, revealing a tiny metal pin in the shape of a wheel. "It's a Pony wheel! I love it!"

"I told him you'd say that."

"I love it, Dodo! Thanks!" Joan looked at the pin again and made another big smile. "Awww" She walked over to the scarf she liked to wear when riding that Gram made and pinned it on. "There, that's good for now. I love it. Thanks DoDo."

"That's from Dad. Here, this is from me." Doris raised one eyebrow and slowly smiled at Joan's excited face as she looked

"Wait a minute!" It was an envelope folded in thirds. "I've had it for a few days. I couldn't even open it; I had Coach open it. He's read it, and then Dad. Now you." Joan's curiosity was piqued as she took the envelope from Doris.

CEREMONY

Joan and her mom completed the necessary forms and paid for the first three semesters of tuition. In just 25 minutes online, transcripts were transferred, applications were electronically signed and submitted, and credits were confirmed. Joan received her student number and an online school library card for her digital textbooks. She also printed a hardcopy card to keep in her wallet, which would come in handy for lab work at Doris' school when needed. The start date for her school was entirely up to her.

Joan had transformed her room into a professional office, painting the window wall with a glossy, warm gold color that she and Doris had chosen from Pa's collection in the shed. They decided gold would be both motivating and uplifting. "Olympic Gold" Joan had mentioned. She had also acquired three large poster boards for various purposes. One was designated to visually track her progress in each course, allowing her to monitor tests and assignments. Another board was divided into three vertical columns, each representing the credits earned throughout each semester. The third board was reserved for visions to create together representing their dreams and aspirations. A vision board. Gram's idea and they were both excited about implementing it. Although Joan wasn't sure what to put on it, she hoped inspiration would strike when they worked on it together.

Joan was feeling nervous, not just about starting her new school but also because Doris would soon be leaving for Texas to undergo three weeks of training with her new coaches, including pre-trials before her school officially began. They would have only a few days together once Doris returned before Joan embarked on her own academic journey. These were crucial moments on the horizon, and the realization that their lives were about to undergo significant change, left her both excited and anxious.

Joan sat in her office chair and reflected on the journey that had brought her to this point. It seemed just yesterday she was confined to her hospital room, enduring what she and Nurse Jane humorously referred to as "lockdown."

As she spun around and around, she thought about her right foot; the grief, the feeling held captive by the healing process. And now liberated and responsible for directing her new-found freedom with the assistance of Pony. The joy she now experienced was beyond anything she had ever imagined. It reminded her of Gram's saying: "Expect the unexpected, and you'll never be disappointed."

Just then, a knock on her room's door frame interrupted her thoughts.

"Okay, Lady Joan, are you ready? I am," Gram's voice announced her presence.

"Yep, sure!" Joan replied, standing up a bit too quickly after all the spinning. She chuckled at her own silliness. "I'll let Doris know we're on our way."

Gram and Joan bundled up, and Gram handed Joan a large basket to carry out to the car. They started Gram's old Pontiac, and a loud screech filled the air.

"Fan Belt," Joan identified the issue. "It just needs a bit of tightening," she said with a smile. Gram nodded and gave Joan a playful elbow nudge.

"We'll take care of it when we get back, sweetheart. Good on you for knowing what that is."

They picked up Doris, who was waiting at the edge of her driveway, and the three headed to the river put-in. The parking lot was adorned with alder leaves whose vibrant colors mingled with the stone-gray rocks, all illuminated by the sunlight. The three women couldn't help but exclaim in awe at the beauty surrounding them as they exited the car.

Gram took the basket from Joan and walked over to the river's edge. She turned and the girls followed her lead. Gram faced them and began to speak.

"First, I want to thank you both for coming. This, ladies, is not just a ladies-only picnic. It's a ceremony for the two of you," Gram announced. The girls stood silently, listening intently.

"You both have entered a significant phase in life, a time when young women transition into independence and step out into the world. Joan, you've been practicing this transition with Pony and your retreats here with the river. Doris, you've been pursuing your independent goals in diving and managing your life this summer with grace and strength, allowing your mother to work her night shifts. Both of you have strong female role models in your lives to look up to and respect. As you grow older your admiration for them will only deepen. Today, it's our turn. River, Rock, Tree, Me, The Elders. To show our recognition and respect to you in the ceremony."

Gram's words carried a sense of importance and gravity. The girls exchanged glances, absorbing the significance of the moment.

"First, let's talk about water," Gram continued, "Water represents the connection that binds us all. All water on Earth is connected, and today, we will bless you with water from the Earth."

Doris was invited to sit by the water, and Gram dipped her hand into the river. *"Anaiden Vinu.* This symbolizes our interconnectedness. No matter where life takes you, you'll always be connected. Whenever you feel alone or in need, find the nearest source of water, connect with it, and you'll never feel alone or lacking. There is a correlation of Consciousness and Water."

Next, Gram turned her attention to Joan, who had taken a seat beside the river as well. "Sometimes, you won't just feel a little lonely or unsupported; you may experience deep sadness. On those days, take a bath and allow your sadness to flow into the water. As the water drains away, let it carry away your sorrows. Allow the healing forces of nature to mend your sadness. Surrender and allow. This is the wisdom of our Female Elders."

The air was filled with a deep sense of understanding and acceptance. The girls absorbed Gram's teachings, feeling a profound connection to nature and to each other.

"*Anaiden Vinu* Joan, Doris," Gram addressed them with warmth and wisdom, "you are both embarking on your first steps into adulthood. Remember that you have each other, your mothers, and me to lean on. Be open with your words, and more importantly. with your ears, minds and hearts. Remember this and remind each other."

A peaceful silence settled over the group as the distant sound of a barking dog echoed down the river. The girls shared a knowing glance, appreciating the significance of this moment.

"Yes," Gram added with a smile, "and let's not forget the wisdom of the females in nature."

The girls laughed in unison, feeling a profound connection not only to each other and their human ancestors but also to the natural world around them.

"Okay ladies," Gram concluded, "I've prepared a carrot cake with icing in a 1:1 ratio. Math that makes sense to me."

"Thank you, Gram," Joan said, standing up and hugging her grandmother. Doris joined in, "Gram sandwich."

"Mmm," Gram responded, "my favorite."

UNLIMITED

When Joan realized that it was just a game of puzzles, Algebra became much easier. She had been up early studying at the kitchen table, now a developed and enjoyable habit she and Pa shared. Joan would rise before Pa, spread her books out, and start the kettle for tea. He would join her quietly, pour himself a cup and sit across from her in his usual spot. They coexisted peacefully sharing a quiet morning meditation.

Pa challenged Joan to achieve all A's, since learning was her intended goal anyway, and offered a trip to a motorcycle museum as a reward for good grades at the end of the quarter. Originally it had been Gram's idea to offer Joan a reward to motivate her, thinking of something much simpler as a reward, like a pie. The motorcycle museum idea was a surprise to Gram, and she knew it was fantastic. This young lady had become all about motorcycles.

Gram entered the kitchen this morning humming a Beatles tune, and Joan frowned at her books even harder. Gram noticed and immediately fell silent. They had an unspoken agreement that they were a team working toward this goal. Everyone's support was crucial, and even Doris knew to give Joan space in the mornings. Doris had once left a small, palm-sized metal bird's wing at the front door with a note that read,

"Good morning, Joan. Like the wings of birds in graceful flight, we lift each other reaching for heights. You've got this!"

Doris had left it there before heading off to diving practice, wearing a bright smile one morning. As Doris pedaled away, she thought about Gram's ceremony and how powerful it had been in its own way. Both she and Joan had felt incredibly focused and empowered. She recalled a quote from Michael Phelps and spoke it aloud as she pumped her pedals, "Don't put a limit on anything. The more you dream, the further you get."

LISTENING

"I can see your grades, but the portal doesn't show me individual test scores, only your overall progress," Joan nodded. The online portal for her program was quite clunky and she was sure they hadn't asked a kid for help when designing or building it. As she jotted down notes in her journal, her mom called.

"I'll send you the link to get you in there; they put the navigation menus on the bottom right which probably confuses everyone. Once you're in there it will make sense. Let me know if you have trouble; I look in there all the time. When they moved me into accelerated it sort of confused the site. There are two places we have to go to get all my information. But no problems; everything is great Mom."

"It's a little busier than usual here Jo. I miss you so much. Sometimes I think it's time to come home. What do you think?"

"I mean, I miss you a lot too Mom, but there's nothing else here. Maybe you're having a time of circling the drain, let's see if we can bubble you up to the surface. We could call each other more often if that would help. The word 'busy' here means that pile of kittens. Nothing happens in town, or nothing yet anyway. It would probably drive you crazy. I'm fine. I'm great really. Everyone here is fine. I think all you need is some of that weird camp karaoke you all do there." Joan made a heart shape with her two hands and imitated it pulsing by pushing and pulling it away from the screen. "I'm all books, and Doris and I are both busy with our goals. She's doing great and calls from colleges wanting her are coming in."

"That's so exciting for her! Dance party? Dance party, let's go!"

"No Mom!" Joan rolled her eyeballs and then her expression turned full circle and she smiled, "I'm so happy for her that my whole body feels like it's squeezing itself!"

"This summer has been a miraculous gift to you. You know kiddo, it's a miracle how far you've come. We all had a long stretch of healing to sit in and you, well you had to swim in the deep end of it all. I'm so proud of you. We all just wanted you to heal." Joan's mom coughed, feeling a tear coming. This was not the time, she thought. "And how have you been?" Joan's mom's tone of voice was so loving it felt like a hug. Joan just sat in a moment of silence while thinking about her answer.

"Pretty good, Mom. There's a smell in the shed, I think it's a wood stain because it's in one spot where there are cans of paints and stains and there is a row of just stains. When I get close and smell it, it triggers a memory and just a little rise happens, but I can control it and back away. It's interesting because I use it to control my reaction, y'know? Just now and then. Like, I'll approach it and close my eyes." Joan closed her eyes to give an example. "And smell it, and at the same time stop me from going down that uhm, like drain of not being here. Instead of it all flooding back in I tell myself I am okay, I am okay, this is a memory, I am fine. I talk to my nervous system." Joan opened her eyes and looked at her mom for some facial hint of disapproval and possible insanity.

"Did someone teach you that?"

"No, it just seems like a good thing, and it seems to be working. I haven't had an episode in months. When I do go to smell that stuff, even though knowing what could happen makes it scary, I do it because it is a little easier to do each time and a little easier each time to control."

"That's an exercise I use in my practice of Energy Transformational Therapy, Joan. What you discovered is part of a technique we use in clinical practices. We used it with your leg pains when you were younger. Those nights when Saturn would wake you—"

"Scream out. It would scream me awake!" Joan interrupted with a headshake. "It screamed. Mom, it was really bad."

"Yes, those nights," Joan's mom bowed her head for a moment, thinking for a flashing moment of thanks of that was then and this is now. She continued, "I would hold you and ask you where it is inside your body that you feel it now, right now. And then I'd ask you to slow down your breathing. Watch your breathing. Just easy, in and out. Acknowledging that there is pain, and when you are ready, to go within and imagine yourself within your body in that area where you feel the pain. Breathing, breathing, breathing. Taking our time. Remember that?"

"Keep going, Mom; then what?" Joan was intently listening, as she had an idea about this exercise and wanted to remember how to do it.

"Okay, I think I have time to—" Joan's mom looked over to her right, then left, for anything pulling her attention away. "Yes, let's do a small session now if you would like that. Do I have permission to work with you and your energy, Joan? It's always important to ask permission before working with another in healing."

Joan nodded," You have my permission, Mom." Which sounded weird to say to her own mom, but she was all in.

Joan's mom continued, "You can practice this with what you're doing in the shed. Okay?"

Joan nodded and closed her eyes. "It will make more sense after we're done, and you go practice on your own. Remember to always begin with a protection prayer of love." She closed her eyes.

"You are safe where you are. I am with you, and we are going to go on a journey together. I will be here above as you now go within your body for a few moments. What's up? Is there any discomfort calling your attention right now? Answer me with your voice when you are ready."

Joan took a deep breath, trusting her mother with her life and knowing she was safe in closing her eyes to look for discomfort within. She listened to her thoughts popping up and asked herself if this was a bother when each one did. The outside of her left elbow was sore from knocking it on the corner of Gram's pantry door left open. Ice cream. The usual discomfort when it was time for her prosthetic socket to get adjusted due to her body growing was beginning to ache. Chocolate chip ice cream, maybe homemade. Then a sharp pain in her right shoulder blade showed up. "Take your time," her mother softly encouraged her.

"I got it, yep. Ooo, Mom, my shoulder blade hurts somewhere. It kind of creeps up my neck for sure. That's what's up right now."

"Good job listening." She heard her mom take soothing deep breaths that sounded intentional for Joan to also breathe, and it reminded Joan to do the same, so she followed. "I want you to travel within your body; imagine yourself, as a tiny Joan that can roam around in the area of your shoulder. Can you do that?" Joan nodded, her eyes still closed, and she was doing just that. But she would change the image from feeling tiny and shrinking down to inches to seeing from outside herself as if watching a film of herself shrinking.

"Allow whatever comes up. If you feel silly or feel you are faking it, that's fine; allow that. That's normal. If you see yourself, or not. Maybe you are the observer, or maybe you are seeing from there as you look around. Take a moment and notice how you are approaching this exercise. Just breathe and allow this exercise to become just what it is for now. No rush," Her mother took another audible breath and offered, "Are you inside your body? Answer me with your voice when you are ready."

"Yes, I am kind of in a cave?" Joan replied, "I mean it's just black, but I know, like, I feel, I'm -inside -something; it must be me? Ah, it's my shoulder area, I don't know how I know that. I—I *feel* it is where I am."

"I want you now to look around. You are going to find the pain. I am with you here, nothing to fear. Walk around if you can, take a breath, walk and look around in the area, asking to see the energy that is the pain in your shoulder."

Joan watched herself from above looking around and then weirdly, she was looking with her own eyes, no longer from above but *within* now. She saw a big boulder-like red ball. "K, I see it."

"Use your voice to describe it to me."

"K. It's big, like, uhm, oblong. Like one of those boulders in Central Park, we'd play on."

"That's great. So, is it complete as one, alone? Or perhaps reaching out to anything? It's okay to walk around it and report in."

"This is cool Mom. Okay, so now it's super shiny and kinda pulsating like it's—uhm—panting? It is by itself. Nothing reaching out. Smooth...yeah, a dark red oval. K. mm."

"Let's take a breath and just be with it. Nothing to do, just be with it in its presence. When you are ready, I'd like you to look for an area where it can speak or communicate with you. Look carefully; it might be talkative or quite shy. You are safe; you are not alone; we are all meeting each other." Joan's mom glanced left and right to be sure she was not going to be interrupted. She breathed into her heart, fortified herself and Joan, and their computers and imagined the pathway between them in a white light of impenetrable protection around them all. She periodically checked around her physical surroundings. Always wise to expect the unexpected, but this felt secure, and she was so happy to be passing this teaching on to Joan.

"Oh okay," Joan said. She was responding out loud to the energy, nodding her head. "He says he's here to teach me, waiting—no, wanting for me to learn something? Yeah, that's what he said. I just felt it nod to me. Whoa, this is wild Mom."

"Yes, it's wild. It's real. You are doing wonderfully. We all are. Now, ask it: 'What is it you'd like me to learn? How can I learn from you?'" Joan's mom closed her eyes, nodding.

Joan was so still and quick to surrender to this inner work. Her mother looked around; no one was demanding her attention. She continued to hold the energy, grounding the session and letting her mind relax. It wandered to remembering back in the hospital when Joan was in terrible pain, and she would talk Joan through breathing and allowing, what Joan would call 'dancing.' She'd call out, "Mom, can we dance with the pain now? It hurts so much!"

"Remember to keep breathing and allow. Be patient for answers and repeat what you hear the energy say.

Usually, once you validate and acknowledge it, more communication comes forth."

Down the hall from Joan's room, Gram was on the couch under the living room window, spread out, propped up, a pillow behind her head, another on her stomach for her book to rest on. She was reading a book called The Hidden Life of Trees and glanced above the pages; something had distracted her. She glanced around the room for a moment and then back to her book.

"Mohhmn," Joan said at last.

"I'm here, Joan," her mother said, taking an audible breath, and Joan followed.

"It's a He and he doesn't have a name and says I can call him whatever I want. He says I chose to make him a He. Interesting, because there is no

He and She, but he says "He" in that—uhm—anyway. Uhm, yeah, so he says I am to relax more about carrying the world on my shoulders. To stop lifting everything up. That I sh—no, not *I*. That it is time to trust that others will help me carry—no—uhm not *carry*. OH, okay, yeah, be responsible. That I should enjoy being a kid, and that's my job…" Joan breathed. "Wait, there's more talking."

Joan's mom closed her eyes, nodding.

Her peers had seen Dee do this before. They knew it was a counseling session going on with someone, not a typical phone call at the phone bank, and respected her space. Sometimes they would wave off someone who would loudly enter the area. A respect for service in all areas came first in their work. It was a different kind of family, and they all believed in taking care of one another on and off work hours.

"Oh, okay." Joan was responding out loud to the energy, nodding her head. "He says he visits to remind me that I call him when I am holding onto something that doesn't serve me. He says my body is like a fleshy, flexible mobile car—no not a car, a vehicle and, rather than being a machine-like Pony I should be more like the river that I visit." A tear fell from Joan's right eye, and she wiped it slowly away. "Wow, that made me cry."

"Do you understand this lesson, Joan? Does it make sense to you, to your core?" Dee asked.

Joan nodded yes.

"Now ask it, 'Is there anything more I need to learn from this pain?" Silence. Joan took a breath. "No," she relayed.

"Joan, take a deep breath; we are almost done. Now thank it for speaking to you today, for showing itself to you, for bringing you to its awareness for this lesson. And now ask it: Would you like to move on? Are you ready to leave my body or transfer to a new energy form of light and higher vibration within me?' What would you like to do? Would you like to transform somewhere else?"

Joan was silent. She nodded, then still, then nodded again. "He said you know what to do Mom. He said ... okay, uhm, well yeah, that's enough," she said.

"Joan, I feel he wants me to bring him out and over and assist in his next transformational form in the light," Dee explained.

"Mom, I don't know what that is," Joan giggled, "but this Blob just got all jumpy, and I feel *happy* that you said that."

"Okay, Honey, we'll need you for one more thing... surrender. Feel his lesson, let go and allow him to move on. Thank him now and feel him as you do, taking in the lesson, repeat to him again the lesson he taught you and breathe. Keep watching him and breathing, allowing, releasing and acknowledging," Dee guided her.

As Dee spoke to Joan, Dee felt her feet within her boots open at their arches. She reminded herself of her energy tapping deep, below the desert, through the Earth's layers, where they then span out, emerging like tree roots, wrapping a couple of huge boulders they settled upon. Next, she checked in on her heart and opened it wider, pumping it full of white light pouring through the top of her head, filling her heart even more, making it brighter and brighter. Only then did she open further and silently call an invitation through the transmission and the love she had for Joan to the energy called pain from Joan. Dee felt it instantly come through her hands that were lightly resting on her keyboard. The energy came up through her left fingers, then hand-wrist and it flowed up to her shoulder, around. and into her heart where it was bathed in pure love. Dee then spoke, "I thank you for your teachings, it is my pleasure to assist you onto the next aspect of your soul. Thank You."

Dee opened her eyes. Joan was smiling and admiring her mom. Joan's face was relaxed as she rubbed her eyes. "Wow Mom, how did you do that?"

"We," Dee corrected with a smile. "Honey, we have been doing that since you were little. You called it dancing with pain." They laughed together, sharing a special connection. "It's fine to cry, and you might cry some more. It's releasing. We'll talk more about that sometime if you want or need to know more. But just let it happen and let it flow for now. I suggest you drink some water and take it easy tonight. I love you."

"Mom, so cool. Yes, I got it. These tears are allowed. That's weird to say, but I understand it." Joan responded with a newfound understanding.

"I want you to drink some water, okay?" Dee suggested. "It will help you assimilate the energies we just worked with. Assist the body, integration, you know. Oh, Joan? How's your shoulder?"

Joan realized that her whole shoulder, neck, and back felt great and relaxed. The pain in her shoulder was completely gone, and she felt lighter. "It's gone, I feel great."

"It might feel even better tomorrow," Dee reassured her. "Okay now... everyone here knows I've been doing my woo-woo stuff, and I think I better go back to being the Doctor they are more comfortable with for now," she said with a wink.

"That was amazing. You're super cool, Mom, thanks! Hey, do you do that over there?" Joan's Mother paused and with a slight nod of her head to the side, she responded, "There's a time and a place for everything, right? Sleep well, Joan, talk soon."

Dee hung up the phone, sat for a moment, and felt thankful for so much. The thought of Joan doing such great work in all areas of her life brought tears to her eyes. Now she was the one wiping her eyes as she got up from the computer terminal. She grabbed her empty coffee mug, and rather than shaking off the emotion, allowed it all to shimmer and swim within her while she walked to the small mess for a refill. Dee exchanged nods with Chantelle, a nurse on her shift heading to the communications tent. As they approached, Chantelle gave a head tilt asking, "All good at home?"

"Yeah. Evolving. Thanks." Dee replied with a high-five exchange, a big exhale and a warm smile.

OPENING UP

Joan discovered that if she removed her prosthetic leg and its padded stocking and turned it over for a long couple of minutes of dunking the socket end into the cool river before reattaching her stump, she was much more comfortable on the hot days. It was time for another adjustment; she had opened and lengthened all and reached their maximum. She had replaced the foam insert herself twice already, and it was time to get re-measured at the clinic. She knew sending her new sizing information wasn't enough; it felt different. She was told her body would change as she grew, and this summer's growth spurt was noticeable enough to be an inspiration for Gram's climbing pea patch in her garden. She made a note in her phone call notebook to talk to her mom about the appointment needed. She'd ride to the clinic herself but knew there was no way her mom would give her permission to ride Pony the hour journey to the ferry and then ride into the city to the clinic. She'd ask her mom about what she needed to know before going, and what to ask. She also scribbled "tattoo," thinking asking for a tattoo on her prosthetic would get a laugh out of her mom and Joan was all about making her mom smile.

No one was around, so she had a full day to herself. No books, her school had ended for summer break. To her, that meant two weeks before her online accelerated school studies started up. She looked carefully on the website but couldn't find anything in the curriculum at her advanced level that would give her easy credits like ArtCamp once provided. Doris had her diving, and school studies were Joan's sport. She was determined to not only catch up academically but to exceed the expectations for her age and family. Anything less, she decided long ago, was a gift to the terrorists who had stolen so much from her and the other families.

She and Doris had been to Feron's, the local thrift store, and had spent the last few nights bidding on a TikTok auction site for creating their own capsule wardrobes of vintage clothes. The two of them had decided since they didn't care much about makeup or fashion, why not create their own style? They pooled their money to share in everything clothing and budgeted money for online clothing auctions. They decided on the 1970s, a time when an entire generation shared their beliefs. Blaise, the mail carrier, told them about when she went to Woodstock. She went, but she and her friends didn't get further than being stuck in the line of cars filling the road that led to the farm.

"It was so crowded!" Blaise recalled. "People just hung out up and down the roads, sleeping in their cars and sitting on their car roofs. I wasn't much older than you." Ever since sharing her story, Blaise would wave the peace sign to Joan and Doris whenever she'd catch their eye or she'd walk to Joan or Doris' doors, adding a "Far Out" or "Right On!"

At the river now, Joan had a tightly crocheted wool poncho she and Doris had won in a grab bag of clothing. They bid a dollar, and no one else joined in. The grab bag was one of their greatest wins yet, consisting of said poncho, two bandana scarves, a white medium men's cotton T-shirt with Kermit the frog holding his banjo in the swamp. Another men's medium thick cotton button-down maroon pinstripe on dark blue, which Doris called "MINE!" the moment she saw it and has been lazily draping over her bathing suit as she went from locker room to pool lately.

In Pony's bag was the cotton "Peter Max" Beatles t-shirt, just in case she needed more as the day wore on. She could smell oil burning off Pony on shore while she waded at the edge, enjoying the sound of the river and wondering what vibrational music it was playing as it flowed, thinking of

Belle and how nice it was to meet her. Pa informed Joan about the pipeline going ahead, across the creek against all those good peoples' advice. At her request, Pa made a list of the gas stations that would be supporting that pipeline so she could know not to support them. Now that the protesters were gone, it was very quiet at what had now become her "sacred space," a term she learned from Tony. He said he has a place in his home that is his "sacred space" and has asked all family and staff to respect his privacy there. No house cleaners. No one. He said he just wanted one place where he could be alone and know that he would stay alone until he chose to re-engage.

"It's crazier now Joan; Tony was in his sacred space as they FaceTime'd, "I'm not even sure if this call isn't being recorded by someone. The AI tech is so advanced now there are videos of what looks just like me giving interviews. It looks so real even though I questioned one of them. Rick, our security we hired full time, yeah, full time now, geez..sorry, anyway Rick caught two girls who had hopped the fence and were swimming in my pool. I did see two girls swimming in the pool that night and just thought it was someone on staff I didn't know, or their friends I hadn't been told about because stuff slips sometimes. But like minutes after I see them, Rick finds me, tells me he has the cops coming to arrest them and wants to know if I want to press charges.

"Did you?"

"No, I just asked if getting caught scared them enough to not come back, and Rick thought so. He's cool, so no, I didn't. But it's like that; a friend of mine is friends with the actor Alek Tyszka, 'Tyz'? Do you know who that is?"

"No, but I could Google—"

"He's like 30-something now, but when he was my age, he was hounded like I am. He and his manager, Hans host a Podcast these days. Mom called him privately to ask for advice a while back. She has me scheduled in. It would get the word out that we are just people and show those who tune in to hear me that I am uncomfortable with that stuff, and I can ask it to stop."

"What kind of stuff?" Joan was super curious now. She knew nothing about fame except the little blurbs like this she'd hear when Tony was talkative and needed to vent. She understood the power of venting. Saturn had her venting a lot when it was the main attraction.

"Oh, Joan. I've had clothes ripped off of me. I've been tackled by excited fans. Photographers have grabbed me. It goes on. Okay, here's one for you: So, imagine this: I'm in the bathroom stall. We have urinals, right? But we also have stalls for when we have to go-you know. I'm in there doing my business and I hear a voice asking for an autograph. I think I'm imagining that to crack myself up but no. I see a pen and a piece of paper slipped under the door and some guy is asking for my autograph. YES, this happened. Imagine. Oh Joan, at an awards ceremony! I think okay, I'm cool here, everyone is in the same boat. Nope. Or I'm all relaxed and then, when it's time to leave, I'm thinking what a great night. And as I am headed, like 20 feet from the door to the car, girls scream my name, and it's like hyenas running at me, and my whole body freezes, then I jump into the car."

Joan went from silent giggle to laughing so hard she tilted away from the camera to really belt out.

"Hey, it's not normal!" I feel like I'm some 'Toy of the Year' for Christmas, and shoppers who have been waiting for 24 hours outside the door come rushing in and fight over the toy, ya know? It's getting worse now that I'm in film."

Joan was wailing with laughter now.

Pa, who was making a small bowl of cottage cheese and mayo looked up at Ma, who was over on the couch now reading her book club's assignement of Michael Pollan's 'How To Change Your Mind,' met each other's eyes and smiled. Pa winked at her.

"Wait, wait, you have to stop. Oh, woohoohoo hold on..." Joan tried to get a hold of herself, but little bursts of laughter kept coming out, like she was cooling down. She hadn't laughed like this outside of old reruns of 'The Carol Burnett Show,' which she would watch with Ma and Pa now and then. It was her favorite. Joan took some fast long breaths.

"So, you need a river! You need a place you can call your own and interact with as I like to do at the river where we met." Yeah, Joan thought, that's just it, he needs someplace more than a room in his house; he needs nature to interact with. "It will settle you and calm you, remember how it felt?"

"Yeah," he replied.

"Well ? "

"I mean I have my family home. Mom's house with my brother and sister. It's comfortable."

"Yeah, that's great, but it's not yours, your own. See? They know all about you and will remind you of your situations, like whenever I saw people I was in the hospital with, I would remember all the bad stuff. It's not a good enough example. Sorry."

"Wait, what hospital?"

"Oh, it's a really long story and—"

"Oh no, after all that, you are not getting out of that so easily. I saw your shiny side at the river. I want to hear the whole story."

And Joan told the whole story about the bombing. He had heard about that and how bad it was. She also shared the news of her dad. Tony listened patiently and she went on about what she remembered: the morning, being excited to be with her dad for the day, stopping first at his office and then blank and black, then being held by the fireman, the loud sirens, shouting, noises, the long bumpy gurney ride, the bright emergency room lights, seeing her mom and the look on her mom's face when she looked down at her. Tony kept listening, and Joan kept talking.

ADJUSTING

"OH MY GOD! WHAT HAPPENED? ARE YOU OKAY?" Joan yelled at her friend's face the moment she opened the door after Doris called back, "Come in."

Doris ignored Joan's comment and walked, carefully, a little tilted to the refrigerator to grab a couple of Pepsi's for them.

"It was cold, early morning practice," Doris winced, having just gotten a tingling sensation traveling up and down the left side of her body, "We were all warming up on the boards, real peaceful and easy, just trying to get warm, nothing fancy. I felt good and was in a twisting 1 1/2. I couldn't pop out of the twist; I just stayed locked up and fell."

"Oh no, crap," Joan said softly while listening. They were seated now. Joan pulled up a kitchen chair to face Doris straight on with all four knees practically touching. Joan was leaning into Doris with a very concerned look on her face. It was challenging for Doris to look back into Joan's immensely intense eyes on an average day, but she surrendered into them today yearning for comfort, and continued her story.

"Yeah, crap... Coach saw it all happen. I was still locked and sort of dog paddling up to the surface. When I got there, he was already at the edge of the pool. He had me stay still right there, then reached over and down into the water, felt my lower back and pulled me up and out by my waist because I couldn't even raise up my arms. Oh, it hurt so much I was crying. So embarrassing."

Joan reached across, placing her hand on the top of Doris' leg and squeezed. "So then, the worst part is, you know that little car he drives?" Doris asked and Joan nodded. "He threw my bike in the tiny back seat and drove me— oh yeah get this, I could feel every little bump as he drove. Each bump was instant pain. There are a lot of bumps from the pool to the hospital —that was a rough ride. Geez Louise—"

"Louise doesn't know anything, go on" Joan offered a smile.

Doris returned with an eye roll and a smile. Doris took a swig of her Pepsi, and the grinding sounds from the metal shop stopped. The silence was welcoming. Joan's nerves were on fire enough already without that as their background noise.

"So, did you go to the hospital or what? You look broken. Do—"

"Sort of, Coach drove me to Dr. Arrott's in his little car. He called my dad and Dad called Mom and we were all on a group call and on route to meet at Docs. We were like, well I was like "Ouch!" and Coach goes "Sorry" and the car would make a noise and jump and I would go "Ouch" and he would go "Sorry." More car noise and after about a hundred times, it was kinda funny. Funny now for sure but then I was crying. Anyway, there's the bumps... and me saying OW!... And then Coach says SORRY... and then my mom says YOU OKAY?... And as my mom is hanging up, my dad gets on the call, and here we go again, 'ouch'... 'sorry'... and my dad is freaking out more than any of us, asking if I hit the board and what else happened, what can he do... anyway, we got there." The ice pack was working, and Doris checked the time. She was told 15 minutes on, 20 off, whenever the pain cycle began.

"What did the Doctor say?"

"Well, the cool thing is, my mom showed up with a shot of something that really helped. Like total relief. Gone. It was like I couldn't take a full breath until then, y'know?" Joan nodded. She knew all right. "Dr. Arrott said this was a really bad spasm, and it will be at least two weeks of nothing. He said NOTHING. And he said AT LEAST... like if I blow it and do things I shouldn't, which means anything. I can't lift anything more than three pounds. And, if I lift something, to do it with two hands and carry it close to my body, it's a whole thing. Anyway, it's only been a day and I'm bored out of my brains. I can't ride over to your house. Lifting my leg hurts. There's no way I can lift it over my seat to ride. Going to the bathroom— you know, squatting to reach the toilet seat is a huge thing. A really slow, painful thing and it's worse getting up— there's a stick in there that I use as a cane to help me back up. I'm a hundred years old now."

Joan was shaking her head the whole time; the sadness in the kitchen was almost tangible. "So, what does it mean to you know—like is two weeks going to hold you? I mean, 'us' back too far or—"

"Ah, the ice is kicking in," Joan nodded. Doris lowered her shoulders and took a deeper breath and another swig of her Pepsi. "I should be okay; everyone agrees. The scans show that my pelvis is tilted and cocked forward a bit more on one side. Arrott said it's common in twisting athletes and that it had been slowly developing and was only a matter of time. We can reverse it, so that's a relief, and get it back in place, but it will take a lot of visits with him. And he said I need to help it reverse, 'Unwind,' he called it. I have a lot of pages of directions with diagrams; I can start when this bad pain begins to go away more. It has already quieted down a little. I'm on an Ice schedule for now."

"I get that, 'quieting down.' Yeah, it can scream, that's for sure, right?" Joan and Doris were looking into each other's eyes, nodding.

"Oof. I thought about you a lot since the pool. I don't know how you did it, Joan. You are amazing," Doris said with a slow, serious tone.

"I had help, a lot of—" Doris' dad knocked his boots on the brush mat and walked into the kitchen.

"Hey, Joan."

"Hi," Joan said as she pointed to Doris and shrugged her shoulders, showing her disbelief and shock.

"And how is our patient doing?"

"I have the ice on."

"Right-e-o," he walked past them to the sink to wash his hands, then returned to kiss the top of Doris' head.

"He's been on me like sunscreen," Doris announced.

Joan chimed in with a positive tone, "Yeah, it's going to take your whole team. Us. I'm all yours. I'm on break. I can spend the night, a few nights if you want that. The less you do the better. Whatever it takes, of course. We must get you better, fast!"

"Dad is sort of—"

"A groovy guy who you adore," he interrupted them.

"Yeah, Dad, I do, I'm just not used to you being around here all the time; it makes me- I mean, I like it but it's not normal and it makes me nervous."

"I get it, believe me," Joan smiled and looked at Doris' dad. "Our patient needs more patience. Everyone drove me crazy for years; don't take it personally, okay, TinMan?"

"Peace," The TinMan held up his fingers, and the girls laughed. "Well, Joan, if you are here for a while, I'd like to run to town for some groceries and pick up some more Biofreeze for Doris." Joan knew Biofreeze well, loved it. She would rub it on Saturn for instant relief at night and still used it. "I have a tube if you can't find it at Don's."

"Right on," he nodded and grabbed a couple of cloth bags and his keys off the wall rack by the door. "B-R-B," and they watched him walk out and down the porch steps.

"Thanks!" Doris called out, suddenly remembering to thank him. "He's been great, really. It's just that he's always checking on me."

"Yeah, I remember. It's like you didn't just hurt yourself but them too. It's a team thing, I guess," Joan lightened the mood. "Okay, so, I'm going to run home and grab some stuff. I'll grab my computer. What else? Pie? Oh, I'll grab some stuff I know you'll like, to make you more comfortable, and you'll need a lot more B vitamins than you're used to having. Google it while I'm gone so I don't have to explain why it helps speed your healing, and I'll tell Ma and Pa what's up, and—oh, you're okay with no one here for a bit? Do you need anything lifted, shifted, brought to you now until I return?"

"Joan, I can practically see your house from here."

"Haha, okay, I guess I'm still in shock. Listen, while I'm gone, you think up one of your quotes for this—" she rose, took a swig of her Pepsi, and put it in the refrigerator door for her return. "B_R_B," she quoted Dodo's dad sarcastically.

"Far out!" Doris replied, and Joan, turning sharply around, laughed, and raised her arm straight up, hand in a fist as she quickly walked away.

JUMP

Doris' mom called out, "Hey-Hey," as she headed to the kitchen with her daily grab bag of empty thermos and Tupperware as usual.

"Hey Mom. We're in here," Doris called out. Doris' mom detoured down the hall and pushed the door to Doris' room open further and saw that Doris was flat on her back, on the floor, with her legs up on the bed.

"As if you were sitting upright in a chair and it fell over backward. 90 degrees at each angle, no pillow, this is the true north for a relaxed back, and we need all the supporting muscles involved to relax," Dr. Arrott explained. It had been 10 days, and they had charted 8 visits to his office, so far. He encouraged her to check in daily by phone or in person, if possible, to phone anytime with questions, and that there are no stupid questions, just stupid answers. "You all are doing a phenomenal job; Doris is healing much faster than I expected. Yesterday's scan shows that you have lifted that pelvis so that it is elevated just fine. You've been eating correctly and doing your exercises, and it shows." Doris, her mom, and Joan were all there and now smiling. "Now, I know I said at least two weeks; we are going to say one more week. That's not a bad thing; it doesn't mean anything more than your individual body's timeline. For now, one more week, and then you can go back to your routine. One more week..." The smiles in his office had turned to frowns. "Hey now, Doris, you are healing much faster than most bodies, and that is because your body is in terrific shape, great response time. We're lucky. YOU are lucky and destined obviously to succeed. I know you like to hear that, right ladies?" Dr. Arrott saw smiles again. "Okay, one more thing. A nutritional reminder that you don't want excess inflammation, so keep sugars low for a while longer, still, and I'd like to attend the first diving practice you return to so please give me a call. He looked at all three of them. "Yes. I want to watch your body twist for a few minutes."

Joan blurted out, "Like Tony, you are a product now."

Dr. Arrott shrugged, not bothering to investigate that comment, and continued, "Coach Dennis has you visualizing?"

"Yes, I have been visualizing for years."

"Great, now the new; you will also visualize the feeling of health and balance within you and incorporate that into your visualizations. Okay?" Dr. Arrott saw confusion on Doris and her mom's face, but Joan smiled and looked around, seeing their confusion.

"I can show you how to go within; it's easy; you'll be great at it," Joan assured Doris, and Doris relaxed, believing her.

"If you have any trouble, just ask, because why?" Dr. Arrott raised his eyebrows, awaiting their answer.

Immediately, without a pause, the three of them smiled, "Because there's no such thing as stupid questions, only stupid answers," and they exchanged a giggle. "Okay then. Go Team Go!" He smiled and opened his office treatment room door and led the way out.

"...And now take a deep breath when you need to see more clearly. It's like a surrender to be seen like you're coming out of hiding—"

"I'm there, I'm looking around, yeah, I'm here."

"K, and that's it, that's how we go in. So maybe feel what it is like to actually feel balanced and all better, healed and all, like ONE, yeah, one?"

"Yeah." Doris was lying there in her 90-degree position in her bedroom.

They had returned from Dr. Arrott's and went right to work; "It's how we roll." They would explain to people.

"I know I'm better; I can see I'm better, yeah, I can do this. Thank you so much." Doris nodded.

"That was fun. That's basically how Mom had me go inside There's more, but you just needed to know how to go within, I think. Do you think?"

"For sure, yeah. I feel more confident again, Joan. I feel ready, even though I have to wait, I feel good. I'm excited!"

"Yeah, just a speed bump, we got this. Y'know I want you to meet Tony—"

"I can't NOOOOOOoooo, I'll get all weird and googly-eyed and freak out. Look, just you saying that is making me sweat."

"You gotta stop." Joan prompted. "He's normal; I keep telling you he's just normal. You're gonna meet him someday and you—"

"He's normal to you because you didn't know who he was when you met him. I practically grew up with him."

"That's just it. You grew up with what he calls his product. That's what you have in common with him. You have to manage yourself as a product, right?" She made quote marks in the air.

Joan let some silence into the room. She knew it would be up to her to talk to Doris about her insecurity. She knew Doris was insecure the moment they met. You can't hide insecurity behind a happy-go-lucky mask of friendliness when you are trying to hide it from someone who knows the core of insecurity. Joan remembered the nurses who were real with her. They told it to her straight, and they were the ones who gave her strength by just thinking about them. There is a lot of power in being real.

"Okay look, listen to me, don't interrupt, just listen. Tony has been doing this practically since diapers. Just think about it in terms of what he can advise us. A personal coach. He'll be able to tell us what to watch out for and how not to be taken advantage of. Our team is here, and we are asking you to approach the takers out there with wisdom and experience. All it can do, at the very least, by chatting with Tony is you'll have more information than you do now. Okay? Let it sink in. It's time now to realize that we need help on how to manage the worldly stuff."

Doris had been nodding along. Joan was right. Doris knew she needed to jump off this cliff; all the others had worked out fine. Facing this fear might not be so hard.

"Just like when you're ready, okay? No big deal. Think of him as our older brother giving us some advice. Think of him as Bob with one 'o'." Joan smiled.

"Bob Withoneo." It's very funny; he's good. Doris smiled and double-lifted her eyebrows to make Joan blush.

HIDE THE MOVIE STAR

"I dunck thatya neek thah-k-jus." Joan mumbled while learning to whistle with her fingers.

"What the heck are you doing?" Tony was on speaker phone in his mom's Range Rover, which they borrowed as part of a car swap exchange to fool the paparazzi. His mom had left the hotel where they had staged a dinner to promote a friend's film screening.

"Oh, sorry, Doris taught me how to whistle with my fingers, and I'm determined to show off tomorrow when I walk by her house like she does with her dad. I want to just be all cool and whistle 'Hello.' It would blow her away."

"She sounds great. I keep waiting for her call. It's crazy, I might have to call you back in a bit if we do another car swap. Remember, never believe what you see or hear about me unless it's me. Like tonight, we had dinner at this hotel, it's a super ritzy place here in L.A. We made sure to act like we were unaware of the paparazzi, and my friend and I had a quick bite, long enough to promote us together. Then his manager and my manager and his agent and my agent all make a bunch of publicity from nothing, but that all turns out as a lot more money for everyone and more butts in seats at my friend's film screening."

"Your life!"

"My life is work and boredom... Oh, and wait, yeah, a lot of sitting in traffic. It's a life of hurrying up and waiting."

"Maybe you need to get away again. You could come visit if you want. I'm not sure about where you'd stay, but people park along the river and camp if you like that sort of thing. I have a lighter load this last year, thanks to the A.P. courses I took last semester. Ma and Pa want to meet you, and we could introduce you to my mom on Skype. It would make her and her friends happy. They're way over there, you'd be safe; no one would know where you are Skyping from. Bring some disguises if you want. You, Doris and I could walk around like the Three Stooges or the Marx Brothers. Haha..." Long pause on the phone, Joan asked, "Hey, are you there?"

"Joan, I have to call you back, sorry. Will you be home in like an hour or so? Hey gotta go-gotta hide, so crazy. Love ya, bye."

Joan's jaw dropped; he just said 'luv ya.' OMG OMG OMG...nooo, it just slipped out, like he's in a hurry, and I'm any friend. I say that to Doris. Cool your jets!

Joan rolled Pony from its corral and headed over to Doris'. She knew she shouldn't, but she was smiling after hearing those words. No cars were there as she rode up and she hoped she'd find Doris doing her exercises or resting.

Doris heard the motorcycle from her bedroom and put her book down. She was reading "OPEN" by Andre Agassi and hadn't stopped since she started it yesterday. She was waiting for Joan because she was ready to meet Tony. She had just been reading about how Andre didn't really enjoy a lot of the tennis he played for many reasons, and a lot of it had to do with his relationships with the sport and correlations about his sport. It was a mess, and if he'd had more information as he grew into his fame, it would have certainly helped.

"Hey, Joan!"

"Hi Dodo, Whatcha been DO-in'? Haha!"

"I'm ready. You know, to meet and talk with Tony if he'd still be willing."

"I just got off the phone with him and he asked about you. If you don't want to FaceTime, it might be easier to—"

"No, I'm ready; it's okay. Thanks, I'll be cool."

"Let's give him an hour and call him. He's doing some weird 'hide from the press thing' in traffic right now," she rolled her eyes.

"Oh, Doris waved Joan off, I know all about that, happens all the time," they laughed.

"Have you done your exercises and visualizations and everything today?"

"Yep."

"Great. So you're like, ready for everything!"

"Yep."

"I think we should start building your website and look into merchandise people could buy to support you. So when you get on the team, you're ready to support those who want to support you. We should talk about it at least and do some numbers, thinking financially building your own sponsorships. If you have the control, you don't need a brand behind you, unless you choose and all that."

"I've taught you well, Jedi," Doris raised her eyebrows.

"YES, I know Star Wars. Doh!" Joan smiled. "I am so happy you are doing so well! Now we need to help someone else. Tony is in over his head. The Tony I met was not who I talked to tonight. This Tony was the Tony that manages Tony. He felt distant, not himself. Trust me. I mentioned he might want to get away and visit, and he was sort of distracted—not because of the Paparazzi, I've heard him around that before, but this was different. I could feel it."

"Maybe he has a girlfriend, and he doesn't know how to be with you as a friend?" Doris winced, raising an eyebrow.

"Nah, Tony would tell me if that was it…This Tony needs an intervention, Doris. We need to rescue him, and he doesn't even know it. We don't know where he's staying in town. When he was here for the river thing, they flew him in; he had a trailer, it wasn't secluded, he had security and assistants, and it wasn't normal. He needs to be normalized like we are, you know?"

"Yeah, you really like this guy, huh?"

"Yeah, I do. Maybe too much, but he needs me as a friend more than anything. He needs us." Joan lowered her chin; it made her sad that he was confusing her. They had grown so close, so fast, and now here was this stuff dragging him away, or down. She didn't know, but it still didn't *feel* like he liked to be. "He needs steadying."

"Okay, let's call him. I don't care if it hasn't been an hour; if he needs us, he'll answer. FACETIME!" Doris ran her hand through her hair. "I'm ready."

"Easy now Sparky; he's just a guy." Joan hit the FaceTime button on her phone and propped it in position using Doris' cushions and her book "Open."

It rang, and Doris' heart started pumping wildly; she couldn't tame it. This was the hottest movie star right now, and she was about to meet him. Forget Bieber, forget Leonardo. Tony was what it was all about. It started with his TV show and guest appearances on other TV shows, and then his fame really went nutso, when the movies started, and the girls went crazy. All ages... Before the second ring, it popped open to a big grin that was more grim than a grin.

"Hii, haha." Tony was sing-songy. "I'm on the floor behind Nick in his car heading to his place. We got sloppy, and I paid for it. I'll be—"

"It's okay now, Olly Olly oxen free, Mr. Movie Star," Nick called out.

"Ooof, ugh, eh." Tony unfolded and sat upright in the back seat. "Hey Joan-OH! You must be Doris!"

"Hi, nice to meet you, Tony, and driver friend guy."

Tony laughed. "Hey, Nick, say hi to Joan and Doris." Tony pushed the phone in front of Nick while he drove. "HI to Joan and Doris, I just rescued our boy, AGAIN. HA!"

Doris was fine and jumped right in. "Hey, can you give the phone to Nick, Tony? We want to talk to Nick." Doris looked at Joan and raised one shoulder; Joan mouthed, 'Yeah.'

Tony handed the phone up to Nick, who pushed it into the corner where the dashboard and window meet. "W'az up?"

"Look, Nick? Tony needs to get away from there, to here. It's that simple. Disguise him as a hot blonde and throw him on a plane. Make it simple. Joan says he needs a river hit. That's what we call it here when we get weird and need a bit of settling down, you know?"

"You're the, no, our diver, right? How cool! I saw some of your stuff on YouTube. My cousin is a diver; she lives with us. She's more like my sister, and when I said Doris, she knew exactly who you were. You're USA's next Olympian, right?"

Doris was shocked. She immediately blushed and leaned back, grabbed a pillow and covered her face with it hiding behind Joan. She lightly screamed into the pillow then sat back up hoping no one noticed she freaked out. She had never been noticed for anything outside of town or the diving meets. She watched a lot of YouTube, and even she hadn't seen anything of herself there. "Uh, yeah. I mean, YES, that's the goal. It hasn't happened yet." She could feel how hot her face had become.

"When then?"

"Well, the team qualifiers and interviews are done. I just need the medical and the official invitation. But in order for them to invite me I need to try out for - Hold on, I see what you're doing here. You're good."

"I tried, buddy, Nick called back to Tony... Okay, hold on—weirdo blue Tesla doing weird stuff—on my six. Okay, go ahead. Waz'up?"

Joan spoke up. "Nick, it's intervention time, and this is the perfect place. If only you and, well, if only the four of us know he's coming here, let's make it happen. We can all camp at the river or camp at Ma and Pa's or Doris'. That doesn't matter now. You can come too... but let's hide the Movie Star and we'll all have fun." Doris and Joan looked at each other; she continued, "I mean, maybe a week or two or even a day or two. I don't know."

Nick nodded. "I like you two."

"Doris and Joan nodded."

"Hey!" Tony called out and then popped up behind Nick, on Nick's shoulder. "When does school start?"

"Nine days."

"Okay. Is it cool with everyone's folks? It can be a real hassle if it gets out. Paparazzi can be hard on people for any bit of information. I don't want to do that to anyone."

"We are sure, but we'll ask about the press problem situation. Ma and Pa can handle anyone, and Doris' dad makes swords so—"

"Swords, hahah! Doris exploded in a burst of laughter, fell back then popped up again "My dad's a metal artist," Doris giggled at Joan.

"I'll make it happen on my end. Hopefully, Nick can too."

"I'M IN!" Nick blurted out and smiled. "MISSION: SAVE THE MOVIE STAR, I'm in."

"Check back with me then, to be sure it's okay. My mom—"

"Your mom is welcome too of course. Everyone is. Your mom probably needs a break too, right?"

Doris jumped in, "There is the Krabill Bed and Breakfast on our side of town and Clark Cabin Rentals upriver where Annie, the owner, just started a glamping business which might be fun. Hotel Coraline, our fanciest around here and it's about 10 minutes away. Bring your bathing suits. Anyway, there is plenty of places to choose from," Doris leaned back again.

Joan smiled at Doris and then back to the screen, "We'll send you links on all this for you and your mom or give her my numbers."

" Huh, yeah, maybe, hope so, I dunno, I—Hey, thanks, I'll ask her. You're so sweet."

"Let's talk tomorrow and make it happen Tony," Doris said with an authoritative tone.

"Doris!" Tony replied with a wave of his finger and a REAL authoritative acting moment that felt real, not just an inflection. "Doris, we need to talk!" He broke character and said, "Hey, I can help you. I wish I'd had someone like Joan when I started this craziness. But yeah, anyway, it would be cool to talk to you and help you with what's about to happen to your life. You don't need to be an actor to have the craziness happen. Being good at what you do draws attention. And you are great. Maybe my mom can help also. I'll warn you about her too." He winked.

Doris almost died when he winked. It's a signature thing he does in all his films, like when Redford says, "Hey." or when Leonardo squints. She moved out of the camera right then.

Joan leaned in, "Talk to you tomorrow. Thanks guys," Joan hit the red button to hang up. She had to; she was about to burst at Doris' reaction.

"WHAT WAS THAT?" Joan asked.

Doris just laughed on and on. She went into a full body clench and her body gave a big all over shake. "Okay, WOW... ok, ok, I'll get used to him. I mean, wow, that just happened, okay, geez, okay... shit, okay. I have to get used to it. My God, you're gonna marry him, and I need to be normal around you guys."

Nick grabbed the phone and handed it over his shoulder. "She's a keeper."

INQUIRE WITHIN

Joan's ride along the river continued through the gentle curves in the road. The purring of Pony's engine matched the soothing feeling of the river creating a symphony of tranquility. The world around her seemed to slow down and she welcomed the sensation of being in sync with the natural flow of life.

As she rode her thoughts meandered through memories of her time with Pony. The freedom and liberation it had brought her were immeasurable. The wind in her hair, the open road, and the bond between rider and machine made for a profound connection that she cherished.

"Thank you," Joan said aloud, her voice carried away by the wind. A simple expression of gratitude for the present moment.

Thoughts ebbed and flowed within her mind like the gentle ripples on the river's surface. She allowed them to come and go without judgment, embracing the serenity of the ride. She knew that sometimes clarity emerged when the mind was at ease.

A gentle knock on Pony's gas tank assured her that they had enough fuel for the journey home. The world passed by in a picturesque blur with nature's artwork on full display.

Joan passed by the oil protesters' camp, which seemed undisturbed and peaceful today. A feeling tugged at her, urging her to venture further north. It was as though the river itself was guiding her.

"I'm following the feeling I'm paying attention to." She thought, trusting her instincts and the subtle cues from her surroundings.

Her mind fell into a tranquil silence, and she realized that her connection with Pony was more than just mechanical; it was a partnership, a bond. She pondered the notion of slowing down, both for herself and for her friend Tony.

"Ah, pace, slowing the pace." She spoke the words aloud, embracing the idea of aligning with the natural rhythm of life. "The pace of nature. Slowing the pace within myself to the pace of nature, or, *not pace,* the pulse. Yeah, slowing his pulse down. His working life's nervous system is running out of control."

Living with Ma and Pa had taught her the value of a simpler, slower pace of life. While the world often seemed to rush around her. Those two maintained their steady stride. She had learned to find her own contentment in it, purring along at 44 miles an hour.

Up ahead, a magnificent spread of madrone and alder trees offered a cool, shaded respite from the sun's warmth. Joan downshifted and leaned to the side, guiding Pony off the road. She dismounted and lifted her helmet, setting it gently on the gas tank with a soft pat to ensure it was secure. She had no intention of getting stuck without fuel again. That had been an embarrassing lesson.

Opening the seat of her trusty companion, she retrieved Stanley, the dented green thermos that had witnessed countless journeys. She took a couple of satisfying gulps from it, savoring the memories it held. The name "Stanley" on the stamped label brought a smile to her face, imagining both Pa and perhaps even her own father having sipped from it during their rides.

Stretching her arms up to the sky, she leaned to the right, then the left, feeling the tension released from her muscles. She unzipped her heavy leather jacket and draped it over Pony's handlebars.

Walking a few steps towards the riverbank, she looked up at the magnificent madrone tree she sat under and whispered, "Thank you." The act of speaking aloud and expressing gratitude had become a comforting ritual for her.

She couldn't help but wonder about the significance of her spoken words. "I'm paying so much attention to my talking out loud, why and to what and what I am saying? Is this MY church?" she mused, pondering the connection between her expressions of gratitude and her inner sense of spirituality.

The night before, Joan had been in the kitchen with Gram, finishing the dishes and setting up her study materials for her challenging AP statistics course. Determined to find interest in the subject, she prepared to dive into her studies.

As she worked, Gram answered the landline phone, her response short and somewhat cryptic. "It takes all kinds to heal all kinds, and I'm kindly asking you to heal. Goodnight." She said before abruptly ending the call.

Joan couldn't help but comment, "God has telemarketers, what's next?"

Gram chuckled. "T-shirts, Joan. Seems like everyone has 'Merch' these days."

The conversation led to Joan's contemplating religion and spirituality. She voiced her confusion about the multitude of religions in the world and the conflicts that often arise from differing beliefs.

Gram listened attentively and then encouraged Joan to explore her own understanding of God or spirituality. She suggested that Joan start by asking herself what God meant to her personally.

With patience and empathy, Gram explained her perspective on God. She didn't envision a traditional image of an old man in the sky but rather saw God as the collective energy of goodness in the world. Her prayers involved sending love, light, and guidance to others, concluding with expressions of gratitude.

Joan resonated with Gram's perspective and wondered if she could use the word "Source" instead of "God." Gram explained that people could interpret the concept of God in their own way, and the choice of words was less important than the sincerity of one's beliefs.

As they continued their conversation, Gram advised Joan to inquire within herself for answers to life's big questions. She emphasized the importance of self-discovery before seeking external answers, given the constant bombardment of beliefs and information from the world.

"I've always liked that we don't watch TV here," Joan remarked. She had relied on television as a distraction and comfort during her hospital stay, but now she appreciated the presence of meaningful conversation and connection in her life.

With their conversation about God and spirituality concluded Gram suggested making homemade vanilla ice cream, a delightful idea that brightened everyone's spirits. Joan's grin matched Pa's excitement as they began the delicious task at hand.

Sitting on the riverbank under the shade of the madrone tree, Joan decided to pray in a way that felt right to her. She closed her eyes, focused on her heart, and began to express her gratitude aloud, addressing the river, the tree, the air, and her current circumstances.

"Thank You... thank you... thanks... thank you... thanks." Joan repeated her words like offerings to the universe.

When her prayer ran its course, she felt a tingling warmth within her, a profound connection to something greater.

As she sat there, basking in the afterglow of her simple yet heartfelt prayer, Joan realized that this, too, could be her way of talking to God—or light. No that's not the name. She pondered names and said aloud "Source...Light.... One." The universe had its own way of responding to her expressions of gratitude and she was content with the sense of fullness it brought.

And so, by the riverbank, surrounded by the beauty of nature and her own inner contemplation, Joan continued her journey of self-discovery, one that would lead her to her own unique path of spirituality and connection with the divine. She knew this was what she wanted. She wanted to learn all she could and to heal others' traumas. She realized and said aloud "I want to be the fireman and carry others out of their pains"

THE CALM

They were sitting atop the sliding hill. The name changes if you're on a bike or cardboard, or if you want to end up like crazy Jon Dickson in the hospital for an entire summer then you swap the cardboard with a block of ice and drag it uphill all the way from LuPois grocery in town by bike then still drag the thing to the top of the steep hill but not just on the dry grassy hill but take it even higher and ride the block of ice like a of luge down the hill's hot metal drainage half pipe. And crazy Jon Dickson was crazy enough for the thrill to go through all that trouble.

"So, who all's coming for sure now?"

"They had to buy more uniforms from Nick's sister, Mary at the company she works for to cover their cover, haha. Tony's assistant, Brian, is bringing Karina. So that's - okay wait," Joan's fingers did the counting while she listed, "A lot we haven't met. They filled the Inn. Okay so, Tony, Anne, Nick, Mary, Lori, Rich, Brian, Stephanie and Cristen? 10, I think? I lost count, it changes a lot. Apparently, it takes an army to save one soldier. Good thing we have the room!

There was silence, and they both watched two dragonflies dance nearby for a moment.

"It's a party." Doris kidded.

"It was Pa's idea to have the workers' thing as a cover story for the group. Because of the oil line, people here are used to groups from corporations passing through to look at who knows what, I guess."

Doris sighed, "Yeah, we really don't have a clue. Look how the oil pipeline snuck in here. I don't think anyone knows about what companies come through here. Who cares about people in company coveralls and a lady in a suit? Pa is so smart."

"Oh man, speaking of that, Do', it's been hard. I have missed you-oh! Joan's eyes rolled, "Just hooking up Tony's mom with Gram and Pa and my mom with Zoom to ask permission and plan everything. I'm glad you weren't there because I was about to lose it with the Boomer Zoom lessons. If you were there, I would have laughed and not looked mature, which-"

"Oh my God." Doris interrupted, "I forgot to ask you how that went. Oh man, that is so big. I'm sorry, Joan! How'd it go? Tell me. Okay, tell me everything." Doris turned to Joan and smiled, lowered her head, and listened.

"Tony said Nick wouldn't let him go alone, even though he warned Tony he'd be bored if he came out here with him. When I met Tony, he said he was famous but not this crazy sex symbol, and an Oscar nominee now."

"Who would ever think we'd know a movie star, an Academy Award nominee even?! Wow." Doris gawked, and Joan reached over, pushing her hand on Joan's leg, then turned-leaning in fast- looked her right in the eyes and said, "Who'd ever think I'd be hanging with a future multi-gold Olympic champion?"

"I see what you did there - switching it again."

"Yeah, relax, remember he's like a brother, he's your brother, just a guy, like a brother." Joan pumped her palm in front of Doris taking an animated deep breath for Doris to follow, "He pops up on my YouTube algorithm now, and I don't know why. I wasted time in that rabbit hole watching stuff about him. So fake. He dissects it for me when I mention something. The clothes he wears, who he's with, his hair, sunglasses. Everything is part of some plan in promotions for his uhm-what does he call i-oh yeah 'product delivery'. Ick, y'know? Can you imagine having a meeting about what you're going to wear when you leave the house?"

"Well, I texted you about the tie-dyed shirt, and we decided to both wear our extra-wide bell bottoms when we head to the B and B, "Doris added and emphasized "TONIGHT."

"Yeah! Couture Goodwill." Joan said in a French accent. "And WHO are YOU wearing?"

"This is streetwear from Feron's Thrift Store." Doris raised a hand up to the sky, "I'm wearing The House of Feron." They laughed. I'm still freaking out a little; I don't want to be all fan girl. I wish I wasn't all weird. It's Tony freakin' Misner!"

"Maybe they're freaked out to meet YOU, you're about to be an Olympic gold medalist." Joan emphasized 'multi.'

Doris replied, "I need a backup plan. Best be safe, right?" Then Doris in her best Joan interpretation added, "Knock on the tank and you won't have to knock on doors."

Joan laughed out loud, "HA! Yeah, that's so true." Joan remembered how embarrassing it was last year when she hadn't bothered to check Pony's tank, and she was out of cell phone range, and her leg was irritating her, and she couldn't help but see a limp in her step through the shadow she followed to the Doku's house where Eric was home and accompanied her back out to Pony with a tank of gas from his barn.

Doris rested her eyes overlooking the cloud shadows over Magny's wheat fields. The clouds seemed to dance along the fields because of the breeze blowing the wheat. "Look at that! I love that."

"It reminds me of Starlings when they do that synchronized stuff, y'know"? Joan said.

"Yeah, it's so relaxing, kinda dreamy making," Doris replied.

They watched the performing art below for a bit longer, and then Doris said "Coach says he has a friend who helps divers going through the program find housing. Dad says he and Mom have been putting away money for my college, and UCSD has already been talking with my mom. I think, yeah, I'm pretty sure, like 95%, that it will be up to me whether I choose UCSD or USC or whoever you and I decide together, maybe we can get our own place?" Doris sneezed, "I started working on my admission letter."

"What do you mean? We know you're in; they want you."

"Yeah. Yeah, sure-sure, so I want you to read it, the letter, when I'm done. I keep it in my locker at the gym for dry-land practice. Whenever Coach goes off on a tangent coaching someone through dive transitions on the tramp it might go on for like an hour so I can work on the letter. I'll grab it and a pen and work on it while stretching."

"That's smart..." Joan was staring at the cloud shadows.

"I thought it would be about my back, y'know - when I hurt it and felt like that was it. But it morphed into You. It's all about you, Joan. About you and how you're coming here to live helped me not only heal my back but really taught me about living and choosing to live and overcome pain and any obstacles like my back, because of what you have done and do... it's a Joan love letter, heh heh."

"Wa-What? That's so sweet! Ooo, I'm famous!" Joan giggled. "Oh yeah, we need to read each other's and rewrite a lot, I bet. We HAVE to do this; it will be so great. Okay, UCSD, USC... I have choices, and really, I don't know what I want to major in, maybe science. Something to do with science, maybe medicine, maybe… for sure not a statistician. I wouldn't be able to hold a job because I'd fall asleep every day." They laughed; she continued, "I wouldn't be able to introduce myself without blowing it and laughing, 'Hello, I'm Joan, Statistician.'" They laughed. "Try that three times fast!" She laughed. "Maybe science. It still feels right. But that's then. Gram says it's more powerful to be present than time travel into the unknown. Which is weird," Joan mused aloud, "because they had us prepping for college when we didn't even know what it was. And now I have the credits to get in early and I don't know why, except to be with you. She paused and cocked her head. Pa says to "Expect the unexpected and celebrate it."

"We got this!" Doris raised her arm, and Joan crossed it. They sat there facing the Western sky. The sun would be setting in a few hours.

"Do we want to visualize for a few minutes before the craziness begins? It looks like the sun is going to set in a while, and I'll wrangle Dad for a ride to the B and B."

"You can dive perfect tens but can't seem to get to the DMV to get us a license."

"Yep... it was a perfect 10." Doris smiled and nodded at Joan.

"How is it going to be okay for us to know people at the cable company? Doris asked.

"Pa figured that out too. Gram made us a pie to greet them with. And it's not weird because they're all friends from the bridge club, and it'll look normal for us to drop in.

"We need Tom Cruise. This is Mission impossible." Doris whispered.

With a laugh, Joan replied, "Do', it's not necessary at all. I mean, once they are in their costumes and they do all their car shifting stuff and dodge everyone all afternoon and Tony has a decoy and disguises, it will be clear sailing once they are on their plane and headed over to Boeing field. Then Jordan picks them up in his seaplane, flys to Port Townsend airport where they have rented out the air museum for a private party event but ho ho oh hello," Joan held air quotes up, "Covid scare, canceled so no one will be around the airport. Tired yet? They have your family van to pile into and then. I'm tired just telling you about it all. We should get back and check texts on progress. He's using a new burner phone too. I could go on and on. What

I SHOULD have done is record the Zoom call to show you. Once Tony's mom and my mom were cool about it, the four of them went on and on about plans, secret this and that. I told Pa to knock on the wall if something goes wrong and they need me and he nodded and winked me away with one of his chin nods, y'know."

"I'm so glad they all get along and this is smooth sailing," Doris said.

"I think so. Getting them all online was like playing with Quantum Entanglement."

"You just like saying that."

"Yeah"

Doris added, "It's a cool name for a band"

"You're right!" Joan laughed.

"Okay, Joan, let's do it, deep breaths..." They both shifted their bodies lying on their backs in the grass to get comfortable. The two of them side by side, Doris visualizing her body in perfect health, feeling in perfect health, and continuing on with her form and entry. Each dive, one by one, at the same pace as it takes to perform.

Her body in perfect alignment upon entry, smashing the physics of the zip entry, no splash. And Joan used these moments to pray, to give thanks, to see the things that need help in the world being helped. She sent love and protection to her mom and her unit abroad and sent love to her dad, whom she pictured now as a long vertical sphere-like glowing light. Gram, Pa, the River, thanks, thanks...Joan drifted off to sleep."

THE STORM

"I'm fine, I'm fine, really. Stah-ahp." Tony pleaded. "It's not nothing." Anne rolled her eyes. "Thank you." Pa handed her an ice pack and water with a shrug. Joan, Ma, Pa, and Anne were all gathered inside the Inn's kitchen while Doris showed the others around the Inn, telling them of its history, and that its guesthouse was once a bowling alley. Doris noticed they all looked wiped out and watched them meander around outside. Nick had briefly debriefed them as to why they were late as he offloaded luggage and bags from the back of the van with Doris' help. Doris listened, feeling excited that they used an underground garage from the back door of a hotel to switch cars, and it continued in a tale that sounded like a scene from a spy movie.

"You're kidding right?"

Nick stopped, looked up at Doris and smiled, "'Crazy to me too. Not kidding, though, and 's okay to laugh at us. We know we're weird."

"Why not take, like, a helicopter?" Doris suggested.

"Why not take a helicopter?" He smiled and rolled his eyes. "DID YOU HEAR THAT? DORIS ASKS WHY NOT TAKE A HELICOPTER?!" Nick shouted in the direction of the front doors where Tony had just been quickly ushered in. "I keep saying we should take a helicopter, but Anne says, 'not while on contract' and—," he was obviously offloading his frustration on bags he pulled out more intensely, "—I say, write it INTO the contracts. Then it starts up again 'bout insurance', and I can't keep up. 'mean she's right, she's great. I'm just tired. Sorry Doris…." Doris was in the backseat of the van, pushing bags to Nick, "How many bags of clothing does a team of Internet cable nerds need for a week?"

"I had wondered that same thing when you all were loading it in the van, I wasn't sure it would all fit." They laughed.

"How 'bout a hand?" Nick called over to the group that had meandered away upon exiting the van. Nick's sister Mary, who looked a lot like Nick, and Doris wanted to ask if they were twins but held back for now, was playing fetch with Buddy, the Inn's pet border collie, while Lori, Brian and Cristen were pointing up. Doris had told them on the ride from the water that tonight was a peak night for the Perseids meteor showers and that they would be able to see them at the Inn. It might be chilly but later is better, and they might want to sleep under the stars.

Behind Doris, they looked at each other, shaking their heads 'no'. "Bugs," she heard someone whisper, and she smiled.

They were all walking over, grabbing this or that bag, and slowly heading towards the Inn's doors. They dropped the bags inside on the circular woven entryway rug and stood there.

Doris knew what a tired body looked like. There's no faking it. She didn't know who would have what room, so she walked them outside for some air to wake them up a bit more and pointed to the giant arched gate decorated with an Orca and Seal.

"My dad made that gate, he's a metal artist." Doris proudly offered before leading them inside to show them the inside floors that used to be the bowling alley around the year 1890s.

"Wow, really, that's cool!" Nick said.

"Yeah, so's my dad, Thanks." Doris smiled at Nick.

"Oh, this will help." Doris found the switch for the porch and driveway lights and flipped it off. "Check this out." She walked a few feet away from the house and looked up. They all did, for a few minutes, but what might have felt like hours to the guests. There was pointing and a few audible 'oos' and 'ahs', and now and then someone would say quickly, "Did-ja see that one?" And answers of glee or disappointment would answer back.

"Tomorrow will be clear again, they say, and if you want, I can take you all and some sleeping bags up on the hill where Joan and I sleep out to watch shooters." She suggested. But no answer. Nick caught Doris' attention with his smile, and then he yawned. Then everyone started yawning and laughing at its contagiousness and more yawning. Lori pleaded, "We have to stop." And followed that with a yawn. They laughed but kept looking up.

"Have you all taken a selfie with these coveralls on yet? This is a good time; you all look wrecked." Doris added with a laugh. "Let's do it!" She said it with a cheerleader's excitement, waving them over, and while they gathered in for the photo, Doris said, "We'll get you all to bed, and then you can sleep in. It'll be REAL quiet. It's beautiful here.

You might hear the stream, and it runs through the back over there. There are a couple of hammocks to hang out. You can follow the stream to the river and go for a swim, fish, tubing."

"I'm just hanging out like you guys; if you want to do stuff, let me know. It's not Hollywood, no red carpets here. We entertain ourselves. A lot of people around here don't watch TV, like that. Real quiet. But we do have the unexpected to discover." Doris was surprised how poetic that sounded to her, and she might have blushed as she thought that, turning forward away from everyone leading on.

Anne had pulled down Tony's coveralls to his waist now, and the arms hung on the sides of the chair looking tired, as if they really had worked all day. Joan thought, noting their pose. He winced when taking his shirt shoulder-high and paused before continuing above his head. Pa pulled the light closer from a corner desk near the door that led to the dining room and held it for a closer look from everyone.

"Just a scratch," Pa said. "Could've been worse."

Anne slowly nodded, and said, "Agree."

Gram had been opening and closing the kitchen cupboards and had retrieved a first aid kit and handed it to Pa, who went to work sterilizing and bandaging. Anne took pictures of the wound with her phone; she thought, just in case this became an incident. Pa asked Tony, "Life's a jungle, eh?"

Tony explained, "I usually see them coming, but the sun was in my eyes. I remember thinking about the sun when 'BAM, this guy came out of nowhere and I was knocked forward into Nick's back, who was in front of me. I was pushed down and sort of rolled. But as I rolled to face him, I rolled on a piece of pipe sticking out of the pavement on the side. Like a cut-off tie-up ring or something. I didn't get a good look at it; Michael had run from our car then and was beating the crap out of the guy when Nick and I ran to the plane to catch the first meet-up with Mom and the girls. It felt like a stab from a rock or something; I couldn't see back there. Nick said I was fine. I'm good."

"I like Nick; he's your bodyguard?"

"Nick's my best friend; we went to school together, my brother from a different mother. Michael is a bodyguard; we thought we were clear at times. Sometimes Nick will take his place, like on this trip. Michael showed him some things. It gives Michael a break from the madness. He deserves it."

"You're very mature for - How old are you?"

"17, 18 in November, Sir," Tony remembered this was the father figure to Joan and deserved the utmost respect.

"Sir. Thank you; call me Pa; everyone does, even Ma -" Pa nodded over in Gram's direction.

"I heard that and I could say something, but I won't," Gram announced, kidding. Gram had taken down plates for everyone, pulled forks from the drawer, and was carefully slicing a fan-favorite Rhubarb Pie. "Joan, why don't you save the entourage from Doris and herd them in here for pie? Best to go to bed sweetly."

Joan had been standing behind Anne, watching over it all.

"K." Joan looked at Tony. "I agree with your mom - sorry - *Anne*. It doesn't look fine; it looks like it hurts a lot." She called out to Gram, "Tony's going to need my piece of pie too, Gram." and took off to find Doris.

"Hey!" She could see some figures walking from the cast of the streetlight around the deer-fenced garden towards the gazebo. Doris called back, "Hey, we were headed for the -"

"Gram made rhubarb pie; come on in, okay?"

"I'm there!" Nick said with enthusiasm and headed towards Joan immediately.

The others turned and followed more slowly. Doris caught up to Joan. "Check this out." and showed her the group selfie. They all looked worn out, Brian and Karina had half-smiles/half-smirk forced looks and Nick's sister and Lori were trying to look freshly smiling. "They are so nice, look at them trying!"

Joan said, "They're all so great, right?"

Doris replied, "They really are. I thought they might be all L.A. snooty, or Hollywood-like, but they're cool. Mary wanted to know where she could get pants like ours. I told her we'd take her to Feron's. I want to make them all mugs from Vistaprint with this picture on one side and something like 'Mission: Tony' and the date or something like that on the back. A goodbye gift that fits our budget. I could put a rush on it on my dad's account, and they'll be here in a few days. For sure before they leave. What do you think?"

"I love it." Joan's heart felt full hearing Doris' words.

THE SUN SHINES WITHIN US ALSO

"This is so great, Jo. We have to do this again, even if just for Nick and Doris, right?" Tony poked Joan's shoulder in jest.

It was obvious to everyone that Nick and Doris had hit it off from their first hello. They had been inseparable since meeting, and Nick had already met both of Doris' parents, having been invited over for dinner by Doris' mom.

"I better stay out of that. Joan softly giggled. "Yeah, I think so."

He reached out and they hugged, comfortably and long, turning their heads in the same direction towards the warm sun. "I'd invite you to come out to our world, but it's nothing compared to this. You live in paradise."

Joan had been walking Nick back to the Inn from watching salmon swim up into the stream's mouth. "Well, if it works out—no, WHEN it works out, we'll be there for school and visits. Ooo maybe we'll need really good disguises too!" Joan laughed. "You really WERE sounding wackadoo. I'm so glad you came and relaxed a bit. Your weird life needs an escape spot, don't you think?"

"Joan, until now Nick has been the only one who I could trust fully, that is, solid." He turned to her, and she turned a little too fast causing a little wobble in her orbit of Saturn. She hopped her leg and settled back down, as he held her while she did. "Like that, like just that, you brought me back to my center." He leaned in and kissed her cheek. His lips were what she first felt. They touched so lightly, and before she knew it, it was over, and he was head and shoulders above her again. They were quiet, and he gently said to the stream aloud, "Was that okay?" Joan, having never been kissed by anyone, any real-life, feely guy, she thought, had no words. So, she squeezed him in a hug and said, "You feel really good." They continued walking, holding hands, slightly swinging them as they chatted, not letting go but lifting both hands when one of them used it to gesture.

"It's not always bad. Really. I was serious about being able to go to the grocery store sometimes." They squeezed each other and kept walking slowly, holding hands.

'The Posse,' a name given to the visitors by Pa, had been settled in for days. Hammocks were swinging with bodies holding books and iPhones. Mary, as Doris guessed correctly, Nick's twin, couldn't get away, nor did it seem she wanted to from Buddy who now either followed her, stayed by her side, or waited for her to come outside.

Tony was left alone by everyone and wasn't catered to, as he had asked. It left a lot of time for Joan and Tony to hang out together. They spent a lot of time at Ma and Pa's. Tony was equally interested in learning about seeds and the propagation of Gram's vegetables as he was in picking Pa's brain about marine construction. How he and his crew built the ferry terminal and fixed all sorts of things. One afternoon Pa showed Tony how to rewire and recondition a waffle iron. He had Tony pick one out of the cupboard in the shed, which held a few stacks of different kinds to choose from. Tony chose an old single-round 1970's style. They finished it off by doing a beautiful job of polishing the chrome and stainless-steel trim. Tony carefully wrapped it to take home as a treasure.

On another afternoon, Joan sat curled up on Gram's favorite upholstered chair while half a peach pie and what looked like a half-gallon of ice cream were slowly but steadily being consumed by the two of them at the kitchen table over a conversation about several brands of motorcycles. But something about the Indian brand stuck and Joan dozed off while they talked about Burt Monroe's

1920 Indian Scout. At one very enthusiastic vocal moment of Tony's, she raised her eyelids just enough to look over and see Pa's expression, then closed them again. Tony, unaware, was what Gram calls "wasting air" and Pa was just nodding and listening politely.

"You're here now." Joan swung their clasped hands, "This is good. It'll always be here. If I'm away at school, don't let that stop you. Ma and Pa love you. What I'm saying is come here anyway if you want to feel centered here. You can stay in my room if I'm away when it happens." Joan felt weird. Was that okay to say? Ick, sorry- "

"Nooo. It's more than okay. Thanks. Actually, you don't know this, but Pa invited me back anytime."

"What, really? When?

"After we bored you to sleep yesterday afternoon. Hey, so I want to invite you, no, Joan, I want to ask you something weird, but I promise we will make it fun. It's a double date with Doris and Nick." Tony paused, knowing he wanted this to be delivered with carefulness Pa advised him to use. Joan was hoping this meant the four of them were going to go to the drive-in three towns over as Doris and Joan planned. The drive-in had been owned by the same family since it was built, and they kept it looking pretty much the same since the late 1950s. Right now, a perfect coincidence, it was playing the blockbuster movie that Tony acted in. She just offered, "Sure." Then smiled. It was apparent that Tony was nervous about asking Joan to go to the movies on a date, and she wanted him to relax.

"Thanks." He laughed a little and sighed, "You're so nice. You don't know what I'm asking yet. I... Joan, I want you to be my date at the Oscars. Do you know what that is? You know it's a big televised, very, very long day and night—the Academy Awards..." Joan heard his voice trail off. Her stomach was calling her within, and she needed a moment within to ask what was happening. She was able to do this quite fast now as she had practiced nightly, sometimes during the day, and always listened when she felt it calling. Like Pa, she learned to follow her own pace, respecting herself so that she could better serve others. She breathed, settled and realized she was fearing the unknown and not celebrating it. She asked her body if it would be okay to let go and let God, assuring her that, like now, she would listen to whatever unexpected was going to happen.

"Yes, I know what the Oscars are. I have no idea what this really is, you are asking me. I have watched bits of it online, but - "

"Don't say 'no' yet, please. I know I am asking a lot. A LOT. It's like, really a four-day weekend. Mom will work out everything with your mom and Gram and Doris' parents. Everyone's invited; we'll put you up on the property — whoever comes. It's far enough ahead to figure out schedules and designers and all that stuff. You will have me there, Nick, the Posse and Mom. You'll be comfortable. But with you there, I could maybe for the first time really enjoy it because — well, it'll be fun to watch you watch all the craziness. I've been talking to Mom about this, and she said she can send you and Doris to her people so you can talk about fashion and makeup stuff. You don't do anything. You just show up and people buzz all around you like bees. I think you and Doris would love it. But Nick isn't going to ask Doris until I hear your answer. There will be weirdness in that it's different, but it becomes funny, making it easy to smile through the whole thing. Yeah, it's weird, but no one needs to know we see humor in it all. Then the actual awards part is amazing. By then, you'll be happy to be sitting down and, I hope, just enjoying the show. I'm going off on this too much. Mom has someone she'll be sending you as your assistant for the whole event and all you do is let her guide you." Joan emerged from within and now felt the excitement Nick had. She smiled and shook her head as she listened with her mouth dropped open in surprise. She quickly replayed the parts she hadn't clearly heard, but her brain caught up now, and she said, "Oh, oh, we have to do this!"

He leaned in for a kiss on her cheek and she turned her face slightly to match his lips. They lifted away from each other, and she pulled him close, kissing him back. She felt little sparks on her lips and when she opened her eyes, he was looking down at her, smiling, just as easily.

"Now I'm excited to go. You just turned something I had been dreading into the best." They continued to walk along the water. The familiar surroundings, and even the light sparkle off the water that she had come to know so well, felt illuminated in a feeling that matched the glow she felt within her heart.

THE PLAN

Anne was just saying Goodbye on WhatsApp with a wink and a Cheshire cat smile. Tony was quickly walking down the upstairs hallway towards her in the blue room. To keep track of the 11 bedrooms in his own house he called them by name rather than location. The Flower Room is named for the large blue couch with whimsical flowers all over it. The Red room had a deep red carpet and maroon framed pictures with similar colored lamps, and so on.

"Hey," Tony said, popping his head through the doorway with a smile, his body following.

"All set!" Anne clapped her hands together and stood up.

"Oh man, this is so great! I'll go check on the girls. Nick is on his way."

"You two are set up upstairs. Hair and makeup. Jamie will travel with us to the theater"

Downstairs in the kitchen, Tony mentioned to Chef how good it smelled as he walked through to the back door leading to the herb garden just off the kitchen and the stone path connecting the pool house to the main house.

Doris and Joan were laughing loudly, and Tony guessed what they were doing. The door was open wide, and he saw Joan on the couch switching back and forth from looking at Doris to the TV and back. Doris was playing Dungeons Of Eternity in the VR headset, and it was casting to the large TV monitor opposite him.

"Yep," Tony said loudly, "I see you are doing just fine. Fun, right?"

"This is amazing. I've heard about it but didn't know it was this great!" Doris yelled, louder than she needed to, above the headset's volume, replying to Tony.

"It makes me dizzy." Joan rolled her eyes. I'm a little sick, but I'll be okay."

"Oh, that happens in the beginning sometimes. If you turn that fan on and have it blowing directly on you, it helps A LOT." He dodged Doris' flailing arms, made his way to the fan and turned it on. "It's a proprioception thing." Then he stepped carefully over to Joan. "You'll feel better in the headset with the fan blowing at you. It's common to feel this way at first."

Tony raised his voice, "Don't stop Doris, big spiders come around that pillar soon. I just run and run until I'm clear enough to use an Invisibility Potion."

"THANKS!" Doris called back.

"There's no hurry. hair and makeup will be with us in the car all the way, so it's okay to be running late. I wanted you to know this because soon, Mom will get nervous for me and if she gets bossy just know it's nothing personal, okay?

Joan locked eyes with Tony. She was at a level of total allowance, surrendering to the wonder of everything she was experiencing. Joan leaned up and forward and kissed Tony's cheek and he replied with a total snuggle making munching sounds as Joan giggled.

"EEEEW! Get a room" Doris laughed, and Tony and Joan laughed. Tony quickly kissed Joan's smile.

"Okay, so here we go, the big day. When Nick gets here, he'll come and say hi and you'll know that it's time for hair and make-up. Lunch will be ready for you anytime you care to pass through the kitchen. It's all grab-and-go today. Your dresses are here, steamed, and all that glamping is done and waiting for you post-hair in the salon walk-in. Mom already checked." Tony wanted to stay and play with them, but he had 4 hours of physical prep waiting for him.

What most people don't know is the numerous hours of prep for award shows. People kind of assume there is a lot of attention, but triple or quadruple that at least. Tony is used to it now, but when he first started the amount of time that was spent looking at his nose hair was not as uncomfortable as it was ridiculous. But necessary when a close-up of your face is 20 feet tall, making your nose a good 4-5 feet. Manicures are important. Three-hour haircuts are usually the day or two before to lessen the chair time. All in all it IS ridiculous but necessary. Tony had briefed the girls on this when they asked for details on the ride home from the airport days before. They had been excellent guests. They kept to themselves and just had the greatest time hanging out.

Anne was in the kitchen sitting on a breakfast bar chair watching the chef work while picking up this and that off the trays that were displayed beautifully along the long spalted maple breakfast bar.

"They're in VR having a blast" Tony reported

"Waze says no traffic and Nick is on route, so everything is on time," Anne said as she popped the second bite of a deviled egg into her mouth. She followed it with a "Mmm! Your deviled eggs are the BEST, Chef Charles!"

"She's going to freak. I already am." Tony, smiling, rubbed his manicured hands together, and pumped a fist.

Nick texted Tony and Anne, announcing he was just a block away.

Anne texted back that the garage was open, and she'd meet them there. The girls were in the pool house.

Nick parked in the garage then pushed the remote to close the garage door. Anne had arrived through the door that connected the large garage to the main house after getting the clearing that the girls were still in the pool house.

"I'm on my way!" Nick said into his phone. He smiled at Anne, gave her shoulders an excited squeeze before jogging past her, into the house looking for Tony.

As the back car door opened, Anne reached her arms out "Oh My God. You're here!" She pulled in a hug. "We are all set; your timing is perfect! Leave your bags and things here for later, they are safe as a vault here and we'll have them in your room soon. Just come with me for now. So exciting!"

Inside the house, Tony and Nick gave each other a two-handed high five, a quick hug, and headed off in different directions.

Tony called over his shoulder to Nick "Hair and makeup is ready, send the girls in-."

"-10 minutes," Nick smiled then added, "A plan is a plan!"

Tony grinned "She's going to freak!" He took the tray of food and drink from Chef Charles and headed towards the stairs, still smiling.

HOME

"I have to get one of those. I think I'll need a steadier Internet connection." Doris was thinking deeply about the VR experience she had just had. It was mind-blowing.

"I can help you get set up. I have a more comfortable headset. I'll show you my setup before you leave so you can try different setups. It's about the comfort"

Joan was doing fine on the stairs. She was shown the elevator but chose the stairs to work out. She was still acclimating to her newer prosthetic. The technology had smoothed out the chunkiness since she had last refitted. If she focused, she had no disruption in her cadence. She was looking forward to Skyping with her mom later tonight to show the house and especially the way the pool was both outdoors and indoors in the 'Barbeque Room' as Tony called it.

"Phew!" Doris took a breath at the top of the stairs.

"Yeah," Nick laughed "It's still huge to me. It's an alien life he lives now but we keep him down to Earth and normal. When he comes to my house, I serve Peanut Butter and Jelly sandwiches with cheese puffs. He loves it.

It's not always like this. Special day, lots of staff, so Chef is on-site."

"Ready ladies?" Nick said loudly and gestured to have them walk ahead of him.

After they passed, he texted Tony "NOW"

Anne was looking multi-tasked and preoccupied, nodding the way toward the salon to the girls with a smile.

They dropped Anne's lead at the same moment, awed by a mural. It was the size of the entire portion of the hallway they were walking through, and it was a life-size Ocean wave

"WHOA! Look at it! "Doris exclaimed

"WOW! Joan agreed "It looks so real. Do you think it's-no, it's a blown-up photo-No! Look! It's painted, look!" She pointed to the lower right where a signature was added beautifully in cursive. They both exchanged jaw-dropping surprise expressions.

They were staring at the ocean wave and pretended to be surfing. Doris got a great photo of Joan where it looked like she was about to be swallowed by the wave and Joan was playing the role of surprise attack upon her. They were laughing when Anne suddenly popped her head out from another door, different from the direction she had walked previously, and the surprise made the girls laugh even more.

Anne smiled, "Lay-dees" she sing-songed for the girls to come forward.

"Oh, sorry!" Joan blushed and quickly walked towards Anne after reaching out and grabbing Doris' hand with a slight yank.

They entered the bedroom, which had been so well refinished as a hair salon that it was like stepping into just that, without any resemblance to a room. They were in awe once again, their heads turning in circles, bodies following and jaws dropping.

"Wow-ow-wow-wow"

"Oh man, man, man" Doris replied.

Two women in white coats with their backs turned were off to the right side of the large room. Heads lowered gathering their tools. There were two swivel seats with lights above them and in front, at each of the two stations, carts of makeup were set to the side wrapped in clear plastic covers.

One of the women turned around, smiling and greeted the young women warmly.

"Hi there, I'm Charlotte-or Char if you want. We are going to have so much fun and it is my goal to blow your minds."

The girls nodded; their jaws still dropped looking around. Nick, Anne and Tony were standing together smiling at them from the door.

"You've succeeded already," Joan said, "Big time."

"Yeah." Doris was nodding, still looking around and shocked at how this looked like a salon, not a bedroom in a house. The other white-coated woman excitedly went to the left and went behind one of the stations. Joan assumed they were early and still getting set up.

"Okay now, let's get you seated. You can put your things here, "she pointed at the countertop below the huge mirror at the front." Joan here and Doris here. Char sidestepped from chair to chair.

Joan and Doris looked at each other with glee. They were feeling the excitement of the big night already and shared the same expression as they sat down. Doris looked back at their onlookers and wondered if they were here for the long run. Joan looked back at Tony, and he winked. She mouthed "Oh Wow," widened her rolling eyes, smiled and mouthed "Thank You." He winked again. She turned back around as the other woman came back out front from the back with her head down looking at the product she was walking back out with as Joan was turning her cell phone off and was carefully placing it to her side. She thought about putting it in front of her on the countertop as suggested but if it vibrated, she would want to grab the call, as it could be her mom, Pa or Gram. Joan looked back into the mirror in front of her and thought she saw her mom for a minute. She looked at Doris and Doris was still smiling at Joan. Joan locked eyes with Doris and couldn't stop smiling.

"Okay let's get started!" Char announced in a celebration and both girls looked straight forward into their assigned mirrors, knowing to be still for what was to become.

Joan's eyes drifted from her own image wondering what was in store for her hairdo to the hairdresser and her heart leaped

"Hi Honey"

Joan's mom was smiling back at her. She was stunned and not sure if this was real-time or-. Joan's mom spun the swivel chair around, and Joan leaped up with instant tears.

Everyone in the room cheered, clapped, laughed and was tearing up right along with them. Joan and her mom were holding each other tightly.

"How-when di- "Joan tried to talk

"Nick just drove me from the airport"

They hadn't let go of each other and were crying again.

"Hellooo Joaneee" Joan thought she heard Gram's voice and looked up to see both Gram and Pa in the doorway. Doris jumped up and hugged them both immediately and then looked at Nick

"What is going on here?!" Joan asked when they locked their eyes.

Nick laughed., "Pa and Gram have been here since yesterday. They were in the East wing hanging out and you two didn't have a clue." Nick laughed. Doris ran to Nick and squeezed him.

"I had a Massage!" Gram smiled and walked into the hug

"Puppy Pile," Pa said with a tear falling down his right cheek and his long arms surrounding the four women, patting and squeezing.

"I'm going in!" Tony exclaimed, smiling at Nick. Nick wiped his eyes, walked over and hugged in.

Anne had been in video mode, capturing it all from the moment Joan and Doris sat down, and was still filming.

It was decided that the young couples would continue with their "Fancy Night" as Pa called it and join the adults for a late dinner with any friends from the industry in tow. "Don't hurry on our account," Pa assured them as they all entered their stretch limousine later that afternoon.

"We'll be in this limo for a long time," Tony announced to the group. "Feel free to text, Skype, Zoom, or whatever." He then shifted his gaze to the elders, smiling at them. "You all can even ride along with us if any of you want.

Like Mom said earlier, it's a long line of limos just waiting to offload costumes," Tony laughed.

"We have our own plans," Anne assured him. Remember Ben has you on the carpet. He'll guide you on what, where, when. Let him do the navigating and thinking. Just have a great time."

"Good Luck now Tony!" Gram cheered on as the final waves were dangling back and forth.

"Oh yeah, ha, I forgot there for a sec, thanks! "Tony settled into the Limo, and he turned to Joan "I haven't been myself since you came down from upstairs."

Joan blushed and air-kissed Tony's sparkling eyes.

"You two!" Nick smiled at Joan and Tony as he bent through the Limo door, took a step to the right and plopped next to Doris. "This is slick. Look at all of this. Let's remember this moment. Selfie!" Nick pulled out his phone and continued, "This could be the calm before the storm if they call your name. And I think they'll call your name."

"I have my award." Tony smiled into Joan's eyes.

The End

www.ingramcontent.com/pod-product-compliance
Lightning Source LLC
Chambersburg PA
CBHW030401020726
47493CB00003B/901